Advance Praise for Benjamin Lytal's

A Map of Tulsa

"Benjamin Lytal understands, and brilliantly captures, how the most aching significance can be wrought from a place, a time, a girl, solely because they were yours. One wouldn't imagine Saul Bellow and Jarvis Cocker as complementary influences, but that's the mad genius of *A Map of Tulsa*, an exhilarating debut unabashedly besotted by home and cheekily, preemptively nostalgic for a youth not yet lost."

—Mark Binelli, author of *Detroit City Is the Place to Be* and *Sacco and Vanzetti Must Die!*

"A hypnotic, near-mythic evocation of a summer in a city and its devastating aftermath. Sentence by sentence, one of the best first novels I've read."

—Karan Mahajan, author of *Family Planning*

"Each sentence a virtuoso sleight of language, Benjamin Lytal's *A Map of Tulsa* hands us nothing less than an unexpected new blueprint of the American soul. Allowing for chambers previously near unexplored in contemporary fiction, it traces the curious corridors of desire between the heartland and the coast, loving and climbing, homesickness and ambition, artists and intellectuals, the loyal and the free. This is fiction of the greatest power and most enduring interest."

—Ida Hattemer-Higgins, author of *The History of History*

PENGUIN BOOKS

A MAP OF TULSA

BENJAMIN LYTAL has written for *The Wall Street Journal*, the *London Review of Books*, the *Los Angeles Times*, *Bookforum, The Believer, McSweeney's, Fence, The Daily Beast,* and *The Nation*. For four years he wrote *The New York Sun*'s "Recent Fiction" column. Originally from Tulsa, Lytal currently lives in Chicago.

A MAP OF TULSA

A Novel

BENJAMIN LYTAL

PENGUIN BOOKS

PENGUIN BOOKS
Published by the Penguin Group
Penguin Group (USA) Inc., 375 Hudson Street,
New York, New York 10014, USA

USA | Canada | UK | Ireland | Australia | New Zealand | India | South Africa | China

Penguin Books Ltd, Registered Offices: 80 Strand, London WC2R 0RL, England
For more information about the Penguin Group visit penguin.com

First published in the United States of America by Viking Penguin,
a member of Penguin Group (USA) Inc., 2013
Published in Penguin Books 2013

LIBRARY OF CONGRESS CATALOGING IN PUBLICATION DATA
Lytal, Benjamin.
A map of Tulsa / Benjamin Lytal.
p. cm.
ISBN 978-0-14-242259-5
1. First loves—Fiction. 2. Tulsa (Okla.)—Fiction. I. Title.
PS3612.Y78M37 2013
813'.6—dc23   2012036711

Printed in the United States of America

1 3 5 7 9 10 8 6 4 2

ALWAYS LEARNING   PEARSON *to my wife*

"Why had Coronado never gone back to Spain,
to his riches and his castles and his king?"

—Willa Cather, *My Ántonia*

A MAP OF TULSA

PART I

1

I remember the heat the day I came home. I leaned my forehead against my parents' picture window and the heat came through the glass. Tulsa. For a few days I drove, sailing south on 169 and coming back, sweeping across on the Broken Arrow, retracing old lines, bearing down with new force. My parents were very kind. But I decided I had to go to the bars.

In the city of my elementary school, and of my good blue-carpeted church, this was a step I had never taken. I knew where to go: across from the Mexican restaurant where my parents now ate after-church lunch there was a row of bars—in Tulsa's warehouse district. They didn't card here. I parked, I could hear my dashboard clock tick. And even as I watched, three teenage girls in peasant dresses filed out of the Blumont and lit their cigarettes. The sun was setting, the brick wall caught fire. The three girls stood there for some reason, as if in front of a firing squad, squinting in the sun.

At college maybe I became conceited about Tulsa,

mentioning at just the right moments that I was raised Southern Baptist, had shot guns recreationally, had been a major Boy Scout—I may have agreed, when people smiled, and pretended that Tulsa was a minor classic, a Western, a bastion of Republican moonshine and a hot-bed, equally, of a kind of honky-tonk bonhomie. Well, there was no bonhomie, that I had ever found: the silence of the suburban front yards washed up right to the roots of the skyscrapers, in Tulsa. In fact I had never seen so many people from my hometown actually talking to each other, and shrieking, as here in this bar.

Uninitiated, having experimented only at the drinks tables of upperclassman parties, I didn't know how to order. "Vodka," I just said.

"And?"

"That's all."

The bartender was careful not to look at me as he set it down.

Situated at my little table, flipping my sketchpad open, I did my pencil in curlicues. On the barstools behind me I had an older man, I imagined him with a comb in his pocket, teasing a pair of women (the shrieking). And a lizard-voiced youth who from the pool table across the room was trying to carry on a conversation with the bar-tender.

"I need a million dollars," the older gentleman was saying. "That's all." And the women shrieked.

I kept my head down. The bar filled up. Dropping a napkin over my sketchpad I rose to get another drink. But sat back down, slowly. I'd seen someone I knew. She sat slumped, looking enviably at home at the Blumont.

She had gone to high school with me. She sat listening to another, smaller girl. While she listened she wore a flat, patient expression, her mouth flat, her eyeballs flat and somewhat skeptical. Her name was going to come to me but I tried to stop it. I wasn't prepared to make friends with this person today. And yet I remembered all about her: who her friends had been, the stairwell where they ate lunch . . .

Edith Altman. Once I remembered her name I stood automatically. "Are you Edith Altman?"

She was.

"I was always with Tom Price," I volunteered, "and Jason Brewster and Ronnie Tisdale." Perversely, I was naming the most unpopular friends I could think of. "Or Rob Pomeroy."

"Rob Pomeroy, the unabomber?"

I smiled, a little stung. "Yeah," I said, "totally. Though I seem to recall that Rob always made fun of the way *I* dressed."

She sort of laughed. Her friend stared.

When I walked into the Blumont the number of people in Tulsa I was eager to hang out with had been zero. To me Tulsa was a handful of coevals from church; a troop of boys from Boy Scouts; and of course four hundred people from Franklin High School. My "group" of high school friends was worthless: an unpopularity klatch, a rump group—we had clung together to survive, but never took any pleasure in each other.

Edith leaned way back, as if something had occurred to her. "You were Emma's boyfriend."

Emma had been the valedictorian.

I think I had been a little famous for the puppy-dog way I followed Emma around, in the last spring of high school. I had no idea where she was this summer, I was happy to tell Edith—probably some internship.

Now I stood managing to look a little bored, with one foot kicked behind me, pretending to balance like a ballerina in front of Edith and her friend.

"Sorry—this is my friend Cam." Edith began to explain who I was. "So Jim was a mystery in high school. Emma started dating him and that was the last we ever saw of her. Nobody knew who Jim was. He refused to hang out with other people."

I was going to turn and go—I was not going to be patronized—while Edith carried on and this girl Cam just sat there patting her bangs. I would leave them alone. I could say that I said hello.

But Edith asked to see my sketchpad. "You should get us some shots," she suggested.

"Read the poems," I called back from the bar, "the drawings are just like, you know, realism! I could take lessons or something!"

When I ordered not simply another vodka, but three "shots," the bartender smiled. He had seen me making friends.

Back at the table, Edith was taking my poems seriously: "These are actually good," she said.

Awkwardly, we didn't do the shots right away. We started talking poets—until, I think, I got too sweeping about whom I did and didn't like, and it was suggested we all take a walk.

"The BOK Tower is so beautiful" is the first thing

I said outside. It had gotten dark, and the skyscrapers floated on the other side of the tracks like magnificent holograms.

Cam, I now learned, was not from Tulsa. She had come home with Edith from college. "Isn't Tulsa weird?" I asked her. "On that side of the tracks, we build up all the skyscrapers, but immediately on this side of the tracks it's nothing but a warehouse district."

"Cam's from Hartford."

"Hartford must be awesome," I said.

Cam pointed across the tracks. "So is that where the cool kids hang out?" Under the shadows, opening out between the skyscrapers, lay a half-dim square, dominated by a huge, clanking flagpole. Moths were visible in the security lights, and we could hear what sounded like skateboards, rolling in the dark. The Center of the Universe, I believed it was called. For its Guinness Records powers of echo. But I had never felt I had permission to show up there.

"Do you guys want to go across?" I asked.

"We were actually thinking we should go dancing."

So we were too old for the Center of the Universe—I assimilated this information painlessly.

Edith—who was trying to entice Cam as much as me—explained that it was Retro Night at the Cain's Ballroom. "It's from Prohibition," she told Cam. "Like the oldest club in Tulsa."

I lifted up one finger. "Can we make a pit stop at the Blumont first?"

"Well, we can get drinks at the Cain's," Edith said. I saw her smile to herself.

I had learned to dance at debate camp, where the pervasive self-consciousness of the smart-kid atmosphere encouraged a freak-out manic dancing, pursued between males, shouting the lyrics in each other's faces. But we never had booze. At college—in college I had briefly taken ballroom. That was it. And at the Cain's I did this crazy foot-stomping dance that I think took my new friends by surprise.

Edith raised her eyebrows. The floor was planks, underpinned with old steel springs—advertised as "the largest spring-loaded dance floor west of the Mississippi." Whenever I stood still I could feel it beneath me, bouncing like a gargantuan mattress.

The Cain's Ballroom was low, square. Its high-wattage sign stuck up iconically beside the overpass, but I had never been inside before. Portraits of Bob Wills and each of his Texas Playboys hung on the wall. Yet in this honky-tonk we had what in the late nineties was called retro music: music from the eighties. Male vocalists partook in the self-regard of staggering, dying villains. They moaned. The female response was tart. Pop. In high school I had relished this music, privately. On earphones. I thought of it as big sister music—I didn't have any siblings, myself.

On the walk over Edith had continued to praise my poems. She had apparently decided she was going to encourage me. I wasn't sure how to take that. In college the point had been to criticize each other's poems. But Edith was way ahead of me, in life. She suddenly stopped dancing and went to grab the belt loop of a tall clean-cut man wearing overalls. "Terry works at the jail," she said, introducing him.

"I love this," said Terry, who kept splaying his hand on his chest and smiling as if he had to catch his breath. "I love this night. I let it all go." Edith whispered something in his ear, and glanced at me.

Her own dance was perfunctory. Head down, the knob of her spine working like a camel. Doing glad-hands, matter-of-fact, meek. Cam pranced up, grabbed Edith's hands, and kissed her. Edith looked sheepish: Cam was already bored with Tulsa, but Edith was trying to entertain her.

The Cain's filled; people came over. Midsong I was introduced to characters who went to Jenks, Union, Broken Arrow. No one from Franklin. I was glad. I liked being the new person. I danced near to Cam—I hoped she appreciated that I too was an alien here. I took recourse to the bar and was back and forth to the bar while our circle kept expanding.

I swallowed each drink and then hurried back for ever more expressive dancing. I panicked when our circle stopped to take a breath, squeezing as a group through a side door into the triangle lot the Cain's owned under the highway. We could hear cars swishing their tails overhead and grumbling on the overpass but with our ears ringing it didn't matter. We shouted in normal voices, though I myself was silent: Edith had so many acquaintances, most of whom didn't even know Cam yet—so introducing Cam was the order of business. Alone, I snuck back in to the sweat and squeak of the club, and I started casually to work. I think I danced like someone who has elapsed his workout and is free in blue space, swimming on the elliptical, an exhausted runner with no particular desire to get off the treadmill. I enjoyed the people around me, and this was a gift. My enthusiasm pinged off the things I admired that I glimpsed in the whirl, the girls, their hair, their boots. There was one cropped-haired boy in heavy leather skirts, spinning. Probably from Catoosa or somewhere. His legs were skinny and he looked like Rimbaud. He probably started putting his makeup on at six and got here early and was the only person from his school who ever even came to Retro Night.

My first plan had been to stay at college that summer. I had applied to work on the summer staff of the college newspaper. However, I did not get on. And no other plan or internship materialized. Anyway, as I laboriously explained to my parents, who were public school teachers, I had meant to spend the lion's share of my days that summer reading, so. I wanted to lay this out for them and wanted them to know that, while I normally would have gotten a summer job, it was better for me to conduct my own independent studies right now, to be at loose ends, to prepare for sophomore year and the choosing of a major. That I didn't get the job on the newspaper disturbed me, but was maybe for the best, I told myself. That there was more to it—that I had drifted, as spring semester waned, failing more and more each day to make any sort of backup plan while this secretly desired home-coming, the default plan, became a reality—I couldn't admit that this was what I had wanted until perhaps at the Cain's Ballroom.

After Edith and her crew came back in, I had to keep to myself, to keep thinking. But the more I kept to myself, turning by half pivots in my dance steps, keeping in time to glance maybe at some girl's eyes, but basically reeling, the more I also wanted to get back outside again, to have another look at Tulsa.

Edith came up to me. "Hey, we might go soon."

On the walk back to our cars a pleasant worn-out quiet obtained. Cam hummed. I hoped for Edith's sake that Cam had perhaps enjoyed herself. We were breezing along. Under the old streetlights the sidewalk was orange, paced with clusters of broken glass and colorless weeds.

I broke the silence: "I love this."

"You looked like you were having a good time in there," said Edith.

I was mute.

Edith continued: "Adrienne Booker's having a birthday party this weekend. Do you want to come to that?"

I remembered an Adrienne, a pale intense girl with a broken nose—I always saw her eating lunch at the picnic table out by the prefabs. Usually alone. She had seemed poor, and yet not—she was always sitting up straight, leonine. I had never followed up or figured out who she was. Something must have happened to her, I thought. I didn't remember her graduating. "She went to Franklin?"

"Yeah. There'll be people you know. Actually the party's at Chase Fitzpatrick's house."

I didn't like the sound of that. I didn't like people who I "knew." Chase Fitzpatrick was a great preppie, insofar as I used that term. I wondered why Edith would be hanging out with him. Or this Adrienne. "Wasn't Adrienne kind of a loner?"

"You know Booker Petroleum?" Edith asked.

"Yeah?"

"Adrienne Booker. She lives on top of the Booker."

"Like the skyscraper?"

"She's kind of disinherited, but still . . ."

I looked ahead of us at Cam, who was so diminutive, and who was zigzagging on down the sidewalk, bored again. She probably thought Tulsa was a trap.

"I think Adrienne would almost like you," Edith said.

I came back to Tulsa that summer for different reasons. To prove that it was empty. And in hopes that it was not. After parting with Edith, I crossed the tracks. All this last week I had been driving, irritably, all over town. But now I had reason to feel I was getting somewhere. As I trudged up the sort of ramp street that led to the Center of the Universe, I heard someone talking. But it turned out to be just two boys, and they didn't hassle me. They sat huddled in the lee of their wall, hoodies up, like old-fashioned wanderers, with the flame for their pipe in their faces. I sat in the wind. I had no accoutrement or explanatory bottle, but I was not embarrassed.

The sound of the boys' lighter scorched up the sides of the buildings. I loved them—these skyscrapers. I had been to grand cities, ones with bigger more crenellated skylines—cities like battleships, bristling with darkness. But it was the simplicity of Tulsa's skyline that had always stumped me.

I remembered on our way back into town as a little

kid I always knew the place to suddenly strain on my seat belt, to catch the skyline swerving into view. This was how I always told myself we were home: like a fanfare of towers, downtown. It was supposed to be our castle.

Oh, we headed downtown for church, or for something like *Disney on Ice,* but the streets were pale, the sidewalks clean; you looked out from the car in vain for anything in the blank street-level walls to tell you Tulsa actually instantiated itself here, centrally. It was dead. It was only way out in the sprawl, in one-story multiplexes, that I ever formed a truly urban ideal, a Chicago or a Boston on-screen with its interlocking traffic and its smooth revolving doors, a downtown that could still swell with pedestrians, jammed and honking—sounds shut off perhaps when upstairs an actress closed the window in an elegant glass-walled penthouse, and the plot began.

That was how I always reserved the idea of such a life (the big city): that it was a lost art. If it existed in Tulsa it was floors above us. Or I saw traces here and there, as with the midtown Cherry Street bars we passed—people outside laughing, guffawing necklaced women—after picking my mom up from night school.

In high school I used to get up from the family supper table: I took my dad's camera as a prop and I went downtown, riding the highway in, to the inner dispersal loop. You exit, retarding yourself down to twenty-five miles per hour on an empty four-lane boulevard; you stop at the useless stoplight, and your idling motor growls— like the monster who's apparently eaten all nearby people, the street is so dead. Perhaps you get out and photograph some graffiti, or a broken window, but mostly the city's not even vandalized, it's just dead. I did once run into another photographer; she was female, wearing a puffy vest. We had both come down to the graveled shore of the reservoir, north of Haskell, when I heard her camera, shuttering, about forty feet upwind of me. She immediately turned away, and I followed her at a distance for several blocks until she got into a car and drove off. And then I flew away, to college. And now I was here again.

2

I showed up to Chase's party on what I thought was the late side. Cars were parked up and down the street so I drove two intersections further to find a space, and then had those two blocks to dally, meandering over people's yards. I poked my head into the shadows of the porches of the big houses, and wondered what it would be like to own one.

I should have arranged to come with Edith, to arrive together—but hadn't wanted to assume. I dreaded the scene. I had thought names like Chase Fitzpatrick's were gone from my brain forever. A popular blond guy, an actor and a prince. A prankster and a rich kid. One heard that Chase was a pornographer—I couldn't even evaluate statements like that. He did do movies, and once got permission to video the empty main hallway over the course of a weekend—which admittedly was kind of inscrutable and cool. But for me Chase was always going to be a guy who drove a new jeep, who stood in a circle with boys from the same families, and spat, ball caps carefully creased, on the high school parking lot. That's what I thought I was walking into.

But the party, as it appeared from two driveways away, suggested something different. The kids looked rakish in the porch light; they didn't have the puff and laundered abundance of Chase's friends; they were slim and jagged, I could smell their hair spray, and cloves. They wouldn't know me. I heard a girl laughing in the dark—fake, cackling, luxuriant. I didn't mind. In my sports coat I was absurdly the authority figure who forgives the teenagers the earnestness of their pink hair and their dog collars: the policeman who has a daughter like that. The policeman calmly makes his way through the crowd.

Inside, however, was full of grown-ups. I was excited. The chandeliers were turned up bright, and amid a crosscurrent of kids men and women in their forties and fifties were talking at a medium volume, standing in groups and pairs indicative of broad interpenetrating acquaintanceship and soft manners. I heard loud dance music coming from another room, but no one seemed to mind. I walked among these grown-ups, contemptuous of their age but envious of their friendship, wondering if any of them wanted to stop me and ask me about something—about college, maybe. Stepping sideways out behind a particularly large man I saw the dessert table: Edith had a piece of cake in her mouth but motioned to me. "Come on," she said, "I have to introduce you to Adrienne."

"Who are all of these people?"

"It's actually Chase's mom has this party every

year, and it always falls on Adrienne's birthday. So kids come too."

"Are Chase and Adrienne related?"

"Their families go way back."

We couldn't find Adrienne in the front part of the house, so we went on an expedition into the back. Edith led me upstairs and down, and the halls ran on forever. Chase lived in a house the size of a small space station—I could have entertained myself had Edith let me alone to look into all the rooms, ones with dormer nooks, one with a telescope, a library, ones with no furniture at all but walls of built-in closets. Alas, one of the downstairs rooms had a home theater, and it was full of kids.

And leaning against the far wall I saw the girl Adrienne. She stood like a statue in the flickering light of the screen. Her broken nose flashed in outline, like a glimpse of what I had remembered: but she looked taller, or was towering somehow; perhaps it was an effect of the light. At the projector, I saw Chase—looking bored—like the bull at the center of his labyrinth. I glanced again at Adrienne: she caught my eye looking.

On-screen: The picture was low-definition, from the seventies. A banquet. Naked young women carted in a large covered dish, stopped, removed the lid, and revealed a platter of different-colored feces. People whooped and clucked, clapping, and I tried to laugh too. I have a toothy grin where I tense up my jaw and bare my teeth, when I'm faking it. I didn't dare look off from the screen. This was of course the kind of movie they watched. Not all of them laughed. Some cringed, some moaned: Edith pretended to

17

throw up. But I stared straight ahead as if nothing had happened. On-screen a flaming match was held to a boy's nipple, and the hand holding the match trembled.

We seemed to be toward the end of a long movie. Something else with shit was happening, but I scanned the audience—I glanced at Adrienne. She was scanning the audience too. She must have seen this movie before. She was surveying her friends in their bucket chairs, an impatient expression on her face. She wasn't as pretty as the Italian girls on-screen, but she was as blond and clear-skinned as the prettiest of them, and seemed—a lot more alive. There was something in Adrienne's face that made me root for her. Against Chase. Naturally assuming she was a captive of Chase.

When the movie flashed "FINE," Adrienne was the first one up; she yanked at the pull-down screen, bending over in excellent jeans, leveraging her small buttocks back as if to ring a bell: she stood up with a glance at the crowd and strode to the back, her blond hair mobile, like plumage. People were applauding the movie. With the lights up, it was nice to see Adrienne in color: in her gray T-shirt, her arms pink. She high-fived Chase, and he captured her hand, holding her while she swayed.

Edith stood me up.

"This is Jim."

"That was a serious movie," I said.

"It was a piece of crap," said Chase. But Adrienne was looking at me. She seemed oddly intent.

Someone burped. Other people had gotten up and were waiting to compliment Adrienne on the movie choice. They were all excited: the movie was banned in the U.S., apparently. Adrienne, whom in high school I'd taken for a social outcast, worked the crowd with a queenly efficiency. Some people got a smile, and that was it. I would have floated out of the room, but Edith made me stay. She had told Adrienne about me, I guessed. Briefly, there was a press. Chase elbowed by with film reels under his arm.

"Why did you pick that for your *birthday*?" a sleepy-looking boy asked Adrienne.

"Maybe it was kind of anti-birthday," I suggested. But no one heard me. Everyone was eager to get out of there and away from that movie. The crush of people fizzed and was gone. A tall egg-shaped man leaned into the room. "Your aunt is leaving." He gave Adrienne a look and disappeared.

Except for Edith and me, Adrienne was now alone. "What was your full name?" she asked me.

"Jim Praley."

"Okay." She took my arm. "Can I take him?"

Edith shooed me away, as if eager to get rid of me.

Adrienne steered me out into the hall. I felt mom-escorted, stiff-armed, institutionalized by these ladies.

"So Jim Praley. Are you having a good time at my party?"

"Well I love these hallways you have," I said.

"They're not really mine."

"Right."

"Why do you love them?"

"Because they seem so abstract."

"Huh. Say more."

"I guess because like the walls are plain, and with this carpeting—like they could be computer-generated, repeating on into forever."

"And you love that."

"Yeah. Like it could all have just come out of your head."

"My head in particular?"

"Doesn't it feel like I'm walking through a hallway in your head?"

She tried to feel. "Yeah. Maybe."

"That's what I love."

She looked concerned and felt the brow of her head.

"Where are we going?" I asked.

"I have to go say goodbye to my aunt. And you have to protect me from her." She looked at me. "The thing is, you go to Lydie's old college."

Except for an ironic glance at my sports coat, her aunt barely noticed me. She was all eyes on Adrienne, smiling over her niece, her bushy middle-aged hair sticking out, her lips appreciative.

"So this was fun!"

"It was fun," Adrienne said. "Most things are fun."

"Okay." Her aunt took this in. She was leaving. In fact her driver had already started the car. "We didn't kill each other!"

"No."

"Rapprochement."

"Rapprochement."

Lydie crossed her fingers and shook them in the air, and climbed into the backseat of her town car.

20

"That was good," Adrienne said, after the car had pulled out of the driveway. "That made a big difference."

"Were you guys fighting?"

"Well, Chase always makes us be nice. At things like this." Adrienne looked at her feet. "Back to the party now?"

Inside, the adults were drifting away. Most had come for a dinner, hosted by Mrs. Fitzpatrick and somebody named Albert Dooney—the egg-shaped man who had summoned Adrienne a second ago and who, I would learn, was a great local impresario. He specialized in youth but was capable of entertaining adults too. Through a door to the dining room I glimpsed a disheveled table loaded with boxed catered cakes slumped over on their doilies, and wineglasses, some still full. But the rest of that night was drinking out of plastic cups.

Under the chandeliers, Adrienne proceeded to command an unceasing rotation of well-wishers. The general mill geared up around her and caught, like a chain. My sense was that she was not intimate with these people—she did not have Edith's hungry gregariousness. Rather, Adrienne had a gift I had learned to observe in college in the very greatest undergraduate politicians: to turn every conversation into a kind of checkup, a set of top-down questions on the person interviewed. She gave nothing of herself—she ended the conversation whenever she liked, and with an air of accomplishment. This is hard to do to your peers. I guessed that maybe not all the other kids liked it. But there seemed to be wide respect for Adrienne.

I had volunteered to bartend, and over the next hour had conversations with a half dozen disconnected people, pouring them drinks—"I don't know how to open this bottle," I said, hilarious. The alcohol made me graceful, and I happily took up position basically manning a keg, passing sloshing cups of beer off to strangers—Adrienne had glanced to say goodbye. A boy with tattooed crosses on his wrists showed me how to prime a new keg, and I started pumping. I was drunk for a while. People came and went, and I asked them for their orders as if I was an old hand, a proprietor at his counter. "What'll you have?!" A guy I barely remembered from freshman year of high school came to relieve me, and I welcomed him like an ancient friend—he didn't have any idea who I was but he seemed pleased enough, accepting my vigorous handshake and obliging my sudden interest in his name and in his Franklin class.

Upstairs I found Edith manning a bay-window bench, a salon at her feet. I swung into the room having forgotten that it was Edith who had invited me or that I owed Edith anything for that. I stretched out beside her and told her all about my doing. "I don't know if I realized this in high school," I said, "but Adrienne Booker's sort of *impressive*." I fingered the curtain philosophically.

Edith stuck out her tongue. "Some boys would say . . . sort of stuck up."

"I'm stuck up too." I gestured out the black window. I was feeling magnificently hollow. "But she's better at it. There's more to it with her."

"Did you meet Lydie?"

I raised my eyebrows and put my arm around Edith's waist. My head was resting on her shoulder. "Yes. Next time I see her I'm going to ask her for her niece's hand in marriage."

Edith shooed away the vodka bottle that Cam, herself half slumped against the bay-window bench, raised up like a friendly elephant, nudging against my leg. I got up and took a cup of Hawaiian Punch instead: "You can taste the huge molecules of NutraSweet, rolling around like brambles in your mouth."

"There are other girls downstairs," said Edith.

"Yes but they're not deep—Adrienne is like a new level."

"You seem like you want more a girlfriend."

I rolled my eyes. "What is more? Is it more girlfriendly to be less like Adrienne? I think Adrienne's pretty nice." I thought I had to account for my being the only male in the room so I went over and put a couch cushion over my face. "I am sorry I feel so like a minotaur I should go to another room."

Eventually I laid my head in Cam's lap. Her thighs were small, and slippery on account of her Chinese pants. So I had to have my head squarely in her lap. "What do you think of these Tulsa kids?" I asked.

"They're a bunch of drunks," Cam said.

"That's why they're so great."

"Do you like being drunk?" she asked.

"I think so. Should I not?"

"Some people hate it the first time."

"Why?" I asked.

23

"They miss having control of themselves."

"When I am sober I have no control. I am forced to just watch myself doing nothing."

The party was never going to end.

At some point, as if it had been raining, it stopped, or something, and the party flowed out back. I discovered a brick terrace beneath my feet, and beyond that was grass, and then great trees. The night air had turned to aloe.

The yards in this neighborhood were vast and irregularly shaped. It was like the trees went on in a continuous great wood, feeding into all the greatest backyards of Tulsa. Maybe they backed out onto Philbrook even. Philbrook was an oilman's palazzo that eons ago had been converted into an art museum, the type of institution to which a field trip might be taken—its grounds, with a long reflecting pool and sloping greenswards, were, in spite of my growing up in a region supposedly rural, the most Arcadian thing I had ever had. We even went to *A Midsummer Night's Dream* there, performed on a summer night. And the back stairs of Chase's porch plashed down into the same swanlike curls as Philbrook's, having the same Italianate elegance that had so taken, apparently, the oil barons who built Tulsa.

I stepped down onto the grass and walked anonymously through shadowy congregations of kids smoking in the dark. Some people ahead of me were skinny-dipping; I wandered further into the woods, in the moonlight, until I came all alone to a huge table, a monolithic piece of patio furniture inlaid with mother-of-pearl, a zodiac design. I stared. As I picked my way back towards the house I almost thought that table had frightened me. I was glad to get back under the yellow light of the windows. Somebody had put out chicken sandwiches, and I ate one, having found a terrace rail where I could sit and sift my thoughts.

The sandwich was good. I guessed I had done well at this party. I thought of Adrienne Booker mainly. Would there be more parties like this, or were there places around town I would run into her? I somehow very much doubted she would go somewhere like Retro Night. But whatever existed out there, I now was into it. Edith would show me. Unless Adrienne occupied a whole higher level, maybe. I had come back down onto the grass and was now testing the lock of a basement door—which opened onto a sturdy flight of steps. With the last part of the sandwich in my cheek, I retreated down these steps and wandered through the basement. I was alert to the creak of floorboards above me: the party went on up there, with me down here, walking on concrete.

Every lightbulb had a little string, which I pulled, leaving them on behind me. It was endless, like an antique storehouse, with paths narrowly uncurled between banks of shrouded furniture. I found an English saddle, moldy but eloquently shaped, like a strenuous black tongue. I noted the boxes and boxes of wineglasses, and the velvet-lined strongboxes, organized with silver: From different grandparents, devolving here? I discovered a terribly real-istic bear mask, made out of what felt like real fur, but with man-made underpinnings, cheeks and chin lined

25

with paisley handkerchief material. And the snout, looking back at me, was lambskin-soft, wrinkled like a glove, tipped with tortoiseshell nostrils.

I put the mask to my face and began walking around like that. Now, this was right: two peepholes to look out from, and the rest furred, as Muppet-foolish as it was scary. I advanced toward a set of indoor stairs, to go up, determined to make a hit.

But someone was coming. At the top, a door knocked open, and suddenly there were lots of voices tumbling down into the basement. I froze. I didn't like getting caught down here. I didn't want to take the mask off. "Hallarghhh," I called, in a jesting, gargling voice.

A troop of five or six people, including both Adrienne and Edith, clumped at the foot of the stairs. Adrienne cocked her head. "What's that?" I decided to remove the mask. Adrienne remembered my name: "Jim."

She looked to Edith, since I was Edith's charge. But Edith appeared doubtful. Adrienne was rippling with curiosity. "What's that mask?"

I turned it around and held it up to Adrienne's face.

She stood there, a slender bear. "You're too tall for it," I said.

People wondered what was happening. Adrienne realized they were waiting. "We're going to take some pills," she told me. "Do you want to share one?"

Chase was not among them, and neither was Cam. I had never taken drugs. "Sure," I said.

Although we were alone in the basement, we all shuffled into an empty side room for added privacy. Edith, who had intuited so much, drew beside me, and would have counseled me on the drug we were taking. But I jerked away from her. They had the pills out on the table. "We'll need a good knife," said Edith, "in order to split Adrienne's pill." I was half ashamed to be obliging Adrienne to share, but didn't want to beg off. "There's a lot of silver down here," I said, and rushed off to get something out of the chests I had discovered. What I happened on though was not a knife but a wicked pair of filigreed scissors, scoop-handled to be used by a fancy lady wearing lots of rings but then stubby in the blades—like a fat-lipped pelican.

"The poultry shears will do it," one boy said, randomly exultant when I brandished the scissors back in the room. People sort of applauded.

But the pills were the powdery kind—like aspirin—and Edith said we should get something more like a box cutter or a straight razor. "Whatever," Adrienne said. She held the pill we were going to share between her fingertips, clamped the scissors over it, and squeezed, holding the whole operation away from her body disdainfully. People inspected the results. Two good crumbs waited, though a significant fraction had been pulverized, and powder was exploded on the floor.

"I'm sure that's enough for me," I put in.

"You should snort it," they said, in reference to the wasted powder. "Put it on your gums."

Adrienne chucked me on the elbow: she wanted to make eye contact while we swallowed our crumbs.

Then everyone, with a ceremony that surprised me,

took their pills and went quiet. We moved the table out of the way and sat down on the dirty concrete floor, and waited.

It was like a séance. We could hear bumps and, much more immediate, some footsteps creaking above us, and occasionally a muffled yelp of some kind.

I realized that the party was going to keep going for a long, long time.

I wondered if, in about five minutes, we were all going to start crawling across the floor and kissing each other.

Then: "I'm feeling it," said one of the boys.

"We should talk about something," said Edith, in her normal impassive voice. But her face was broken out in a rictus of ecstasy.

Soon the room was ballistic with chatter. There was a piano, somewhere down here. Somebody was going to play. We were going to be able to enjoy the experience "without anyone else interrupting."

I assumed that my pill was having its effect as well but that I was so inhibited, and so inexperienced, that I did not realize it—I would have to figure out how to pick out some subtle inkling and jockey it up into my cerebrum:

Adrienne had squatted down next to me. She was nimble. "We may not have gotten enough to feel it," she said. She was anxious, as if I was the customer.

"It's fine," I wanted to assure her, "even a half feeling—I'm just glad for the experience."

"Sometimes you need the full thing . . ." She gestured, inarticulate.

"Like to trigger it?"

She opened her palms, in a gesture of revelation.

"Maybe it would be better if it didn't work," I said. "I wanted to talk to you."

"Yes?"

I had no idea what I was going to say next. "I found some stuff in the backyard," I managed. "We could go look at it."

She thought, nodded slowly, and rose.

The others would have made a fuss had they found out our pill didn't work. Who knows what they did think. Adrienne stood me up by the hand and pulled me out of the room.

We climbed up the stairs and out the door, onto the grass. "It's somewhere," I said, and we jogged into the woods. We had to slow, and start walking; it was dark. I spotted the stone table. "It was in the moonlight earlier." I took out the tiny LED flashlight my mother had given me, the kind that links to your key chain—"To get to your car at night," my mother had said.

I waved the light at the table's reflective inlay. "It's a zodiac, but not our typical Greek one." I shone the light on a round of figures, a peacock, a crab, a priapic chef—

"What's that thing?" She nicked away my key chain, as simple as a thief.

The device was triangular, like a guitar pick. When you pressed on it, an LED ignited beneath the translucent blue plastic and a beam of light flew out.

"I should paint this," she said.

"What?"

She closed her eyes, smashing the blue light in front of one eyelid, and then the other.

I tried to think what painterly techniques would come into play. "It would be incredibly hard to get the effect right," I said.

Adrienne wasn't paying attention.

"It's an alien eyeball," I said.

She fondled the key chain. "It *is* an eye."

"So you paint?"

She looked toward the house. "I *want* to be a painter," she said.

We lay down on the table and were staring up at the leaves and stars. Of course Adrienne had seen all this before, this table, she was a regular in this house. "Do you need to go back to the party?" I asked.

"No." It was like five minutes passed. "Also I want to be a priest," she said. Her voice was like sand. "I took a personality test and it said I had the three attributes. Faith, dignity, and zeal."

I looked to see if she was kidding. But she *was* dignified. Even lolling her head, abstracted.

"This thing we're on is like a cromlech," I said.

"What's that?"

"An ancient druidic, like, sacrificial table."

"Edith said you were a poet."

"I *want* to be."

Adrienne sat up. "Tell me why."

She was prepared to take me seriously, if I wanted. I tried to think. "I want to be a poet so that I can actually write good poetry," I said. "I want to be very good."

She nodded. "Because you think you already are, right?"

"Yeah."

A long moment passed. We both lay in the dark. When the wind blew, we could hear the leaves whispering all around us, but we couldn't see them.

Adrienne turned to me. "When you think about your work . . . are you frightened?"

"No. But I know what you mean. I will be someday."

"Yeah." Casually darting, Adrienne got up and walked away from the table. "Come on," she said.

We walked deeper into the trees, until we stood at Chase's back fence. The next house behind slowly became visible. It was taking on shape, an imposing outline against the just-blueing sky.

"Do you want to go over?" she asked.

"You know them?"

"No."

I had to haul myself over—to be so athletic was a strange breakthrough, on top of everything else.

She walked ahead of me on the neighbor's lawn. It looked like in a silent movie when they film night scenes in the day. An elegant woman at a garden party—until she looked back at me and acknowledged the thrill of it. I ran to catch up. "Do you want to swim?"

I considered: if she wanted to swim, what that would mean. But she seemed up for something else as well.

"I want to keep going over fences," I said.

We traveled laterally, crossing over into another backyard, and another. Each one was like its own aquarium, planted with its owner's choice of plant, ornamented with its own plastic castle, or gazebo, or jungle gym, sunk in its own blue. I thought of the home owners I knew, people's parents. There was something pitiful about backyards, people having them. The notion that they were private. "We're running through people's dreams," I called to Adrienne. "Like cycling through them while they're asleep."

We were literally running, alert to each yard's obstacles, deerlike, but sufficiently full-tilt to make ordinary conversation impossible; some people talk while they jog—it was all we could do to lash out with second-by-second commentary, streaming flayed ribbons of conversation behind us.

A light came on and we instinctively dove into the grass. I remember it was a set of big bay windows, we saw a woman in silhouette, as if in a lightning strike, her hand attached to the pull-chain. I remember trumpet vine, and a wooden lattice with a hooped garden hose. We looked at each other, and immediately got up running. I ran on; I made no silent apology to the home owner.

I was helping her up a poured concrete wall, molded with pillars. "We should break into one of them," she said. "Don't you think?"

"We probably should." I pictured an unlocked back door, a narrow hall, with faintly visible photographs on the walls, like a museum. And then opening a refrigerator to steal orange juice and being afraid of the light that spilled out.

But we kept running. It was obvious, I think from the way the air smelled, that morning would be coming soon. In the next yard we stopped, as if in celebration of something. Adrienne's eyes were big, her shoulders thrown back, breathing.

I spoke: "I wonder if we can get to Philbrook through these yards."

"What?"

"I think it's on this block."

"I don't know Jim—I'm lost." She came out with this very nonchalantly and grabbed my shirt and pulled me onwards. My jacket, I realized. My jacket was streaked with grass. My parents had bought it for me to go to college.

"Come on," she was already saying—we squatted down in some mulch and hunched our way underneath the branches of a low-hanging cherry tree, waddling into a kind of bower someone had anciently built, with hedges planted on two sides for privacy. There was memorably a birdbath. She rocked back and forth where she was squatting and then stuck out both arms and pushed me over into the dirt-grass.

On top of me, Adrienne was neither lascivious nor chaste; she was simply very straightforward. She unbuttoned my fly like untying a shoe. She was quick. I was so in awe of her that I forgot to kiss back. She moved her lips from place to place with methodical deliberateness. She was a type of partner new to me. And half the sucking that I did was just buying time. Anyway she got bored and yanked my pants off. It was light now, not very, but enough for me to see our nakedness in true color. She was whiter than me. She maintained herself on top of me, and had the stage presence to let me totally imprint on her as being the image of the memory we were making, limp back, chin raised, neck red.

It reached into my fundamental idea of "morning" and messed it up; we rolled over. I was on top. "You have to come on the grass," she said. But I was not going to come. I was too excited.

The sounds Adrienne was making seemed connected up to a story I hadn't followed. I couldn't tell if she was faking it or not. She probably just loved to make noise.

We finally stopped. She looked into my eyes, greedily aware of what she had done. Dogs were barking somewhere.

"I think the dogs are coming this way," I said. I had to recover some sense of my voice. She didn't reply. She grasped me so suddenly it hurt. I was intimidated, and she laughed. One thing I could do was I crawled back on top of her and so she had to let go.

"Your arms are getting dirty," I said. I felt the breeze on my hip.

We continued for a long time, silently now. The sun was rising over the people's back wall, and I was the one raising it. It got brighter and warmer the more I went. I always think about this of course. I have tried to measure the added amount of that second time, and how much it accounted for. I want to know whether I won Adrienne, or just lucked into her. I try to measure it when I listen to slow music, and I compare it to that music. It is like the music might stop, if I listen hard enough. When I look at cold statues I remember the sweat on Adrienne's chest. She was not loud that second time, she was intent, and she looked into my eyes so much that we suddenly became friends. I started laughing. It seemed like a place to stop.

It was because of the birds chirruping right above us

that I had started laughing. "You have to go," she whispered.

"Can't we hide here?" I asked, taking her hand.

She suited up and stood waiting as I tucked in my shirt. She led me out straight by the people's back windows and around the side of their house.

"Is this okay?"

We came out on open lawn, in the sun, on a quiet street. It wasn't even clear which house this lawn belonged to, these houses were so far apart and the lawns were continuous—and in the morning humidity I could hear the *brrrum* of a central AC start up. I wished that we could get inside one of the houses. I would have liked to sit on someone's nice furniture and drink orange juice.

"Do you know where we are?" I asked.

"You go now." She smiled.

"Won't you walk me to my car?"

"Nope." She was already backing away, going in the other direction.

I waved, stiffly. She drew herself up and patted the air between us, pushing me off like a boat.

For the first block not one car passed, but then on the next street there were two or three. Did they realize? The dew was burning off the yards I passed, and if I stretched my arm out over the grass, I could feel the waves of heat. It smelled sour. I found Philbrook; I was going to hop the wall and invade the grounds except I had to pee. And I didn't want to desecrate anything. My parents would be on their way to church by now, I calculated. I would drive home, but I would have to wait an hour or two before they came back and I could confront them. So I drove

35

slowly. I stopped at a QuikTrip, to use the bathroom. It was over-air-conditioned and smelled like tile cleaner. Wherever I had left the bear mask, I mused, I did not know—I thought of that house I had been in as an intricate novel, one I had read too fast but could unwind, later, and rethink, in my notebooks. I dried my hands and rushed out into the main part of the convenience store, and fixed myself an amaretto cappuccino, and with the clerk I counted out my bills audibly, like my father sometimes did.

3

I did not assume it was a repeatable experience. Running through the backyards, pretending I was high—bounding after her like I did—maybe I was high. I was grateful that it had finally happened to me—a sense of moment that bore me in my car like a heavy, Wagnerian music. Full of foreboding of course. When my parents got home from church my mom wouldn't look me in the eye. She put down her purse. With no prologue she told me that "you have to be safe"—and that was going to be all. But stupidly, stupidly, I brought up Chase's address. Mom might think I had been rolling insensate on the floor of the Cain's Ballroom. But Maple Ridge, I told her. I thought the intimation of wealth might be explanatory—rich people's parties are different, they go on longer—they're unashamed of themselves—

"You don't know those people, Jim."

She almost never snapped at me like that. I slept through the afternoon, grinding my teeth, and got out of dinner by going off to the movies. At the concession I just purchased a Coke and a piece of pizza in a triangular box and sat through the movie tripping out on my own headache. It was dark when I walked back out into the sticky parking lot. I spent the night sitting up Indian-style in my bed, with my window cracked against the air-conditioning, reading. I filled up a small notepad with notes.

I went to the downtown library the next day—ever since I got home from school I had been making almost daily trips to the library, to try to follow the reading course I had set for myself. It was wholesome. My particular books smelled good. Classics that had been re-printed, they had tight, bright pages, and didn't seem to have been consulted much. For probably two hours that afternoon I took the most meticulous notes—but then got the idea to call Edith. I could simply ask for Adrienne's phone number. Why not? I went down to the circulation desk, where they had a pay phone.

Edith was cautious.

"You guys had a good time on Saturday?"

"Well, yeah."

"Just don't be surprised if she doesn't call you back."

"Why—did she say something?"

"No. But Adrienne's hard." I heard diplomacy in Edith's voice. "I hope I didn't give you the wrong idea, Jim. Adrienne doesn't really date people, you know."

What Edith maybe didn't understand was the intuitive validity of my interest: that simply I ought to get what I want. Wanting was a form of virtue, especially when you wanted challenging things. That's how my world worked. It was how I had gotten into college. What more comprehensive validation was there of a teenager's intuitive sense of his future than the positive return he gets on a list of his accomplishments mailed off to authorities on the East Coast? I said to Edith, "I think you are meant to give me her number."

Edith gave it. But she spent the rest of the conversation trying to get me to go to Retro Night on Wednesday. "Last week you had a blast."

I called Adrienne from the same pay phone. My voice mail went like this: "Hey Adrienne, this is Jim. I don't think I ever said happy birthday to you, so I wanted to say that. I forgot to get your number but Edith gave it to me. Let's hang out sometime."

The next morning, at home, I tried again. I did my second voice mail in a different voice. To prepare I sat still for ten or fifteen minutes until finally I took the cordless like a chalice to my lips, dialed with my thumbs, and spoke: "Hey Adrienne, this is Jim Praley." I paused. "I want to wander around in the night some." I was speaking gravely, trembling, trying to be ironic. "Edith said you don't talk on the phone much but I don't really want to talk on the phone either. However. I'm calling to say: write me a letter." And I actually gave her my parents' street address and zip code. A pause. "Let's talk face-to-face, I mean."

I came from a family of teachers, women and men who had stayed inside the loops of their own educations and flourished, women and men who could expect to rule their own classrooms and to supervise their own lives. Whereas I was trying to force myself on Adrienne

Booker of the Booker family. I went to Office Depot and purchased manila envelopes, and assembled a file marked FOLLOW-UP MATERIALS, mostly xeroxed from library books about Stonehenge and photos of gardens—eighteenth-century Romantic gardens with ruins and broken-down walls—along with one or two maps of Tulsa. I sat at a reading carrel and cut up the xeroxes with the maps so the different gardens appeared to be located in Tulsa. And, in an attempt to be erotic, I looked up pictures of human and animal sacrifice. Thinking of course about the stone table or cromlech on which we had sat. But I decided not to put the illustrations of human sacrifice in, after all. I sat down on the rim of a potted fern, pleased with my efficiency. This was the grandest day I had ever had at the library—it was the payoff of the last two weeks I had spent here, studying, that I was able to zip around so expertly in the stacks. I wanted only one more element in my file, something to make it seem fun. It would be in good taste to insert something that was also a non sequitur. I grabbed a book on Corvettes, and paid to xerox them in color.

This, I thought as I assembled the packet, was something I was good at.

In front of Chase's house, at six o'clock on a summer afternoon, there was heat coming off the walk, and the knocker was soft to the touch. Nothing was as I remembered it. As I waited I pictured Chase coming from deep in the house, his curious, sleepy-looking head peeking out from behind the door. But it was a lady who swept open the door—it was Chase's mom. She was a lot younger than mine. Her hair was pulled back super-tight.

She was blinking, almost satirical when she inspected the packet. Or like she was touched. "Adrienne doesn't live here, you know."

"Will you please see that this gets to her?"

I waited three days. Adrienne called me on Friday. "What are you doing tonight?"

She wanted me to pick her up at the Booker in two hours.

I had to ask my mom which building it was.

I needn't have asked—the Booker was as I had hoped the cool one, the skyscraper with the terra-cotta façade, an eye-swim, with carvings running up like tendrils of lightning bolts tumbling upward. The doorman looked at me doubtfully. I had come in my prized threadbare T-shirt. I sat down on a bench and threw my shoulders back. The elevator was mum, but I waited for Adrienne's emergence: to show this doorman how little he knew of the world, that there were kids who dressed just like me who lived in this building—the elevator doors slid apart and Adrienne emerged wearing a cerulean dress. She put out her bare arm: I was embarrassed, and she raised me up. The doorman glanced at me as if to say, Do you have a clue?

There was something promlike about it—being downtown with a girl in a dress. "We're going to Stars," she said. "We'll have to drive. Do you know it?"

Stars was a gay bar, she told me. "Don't worry, they'll love you."

The rattling, windswept highway offered no help—the city lights had gone silent, and looked awesomely strewn.

I couldn't say much. Next time, I thought, bring booze. Adrienne smushed her fingertip into the lock of my glove compartment and twisted, as if her finger were a key. I never once, all that summer, believed Adrienne cared about money, my not having any. But I cared. My car felt too flimsy for her.

"Tulsa's like a ghost town," I said.

"Have you been to Elgin?"

"The street?"

"No, it's a real ghost town. It's in Kansas. You should go. There's like an abandoned soda fountain and houses without doors and you can walk in." Adrienne had met the caretaker, a retiree from the area who spent his summers mowing the lots and the sidewalk strips of Elgin.

"You know the source of the word *Elgin*?" I asked. "The Elgin Marbles. They're actually stripped off the walls of the Acropolis. Which is like the ultimate ghost town. I guess as a direct thing the street is named after the place in Kansas. Either way. Downtown's so dead."

Past experience had conditioned me to gripe about Tulsa: we all do it. But Adrienne was bored by my reference to downtown being dead. "I live there, you know." Maybe she was just putting on umbrage for fun. But for the next five minutes I was reduced to glancing at her reflection in the windshield: maybe she thought she was making a big mistake.

I hadn't ever been to a gay bar anywhere. In Boston or New York I would have been ready, that would have been my cosmopolitan duty. But to go to one here was none of

42

my business. I assumed the gay bars of Tulsa were fake, extra-faggy places, not gay really but pretending to be gay. With pink walls and Irish lace and super-self-conscious patrons. It was a slap in the face for a "date."

I drove out to the airport, and she directed me to a strip mall across the road from the FedEx loading dock. Three neon stars glowed like mock sheriff badges above stucco walls. We went in: it smelled like fake smoke. Adrienne alighted on a table and asked for two of the specials. We were right on the floor, a tiled platform where a line dance was forming. Everything was pretty random—big-bulb Christmas lights on the bar, fake palm trees at each corner of the dance floor, and a DJ booth set up under a fake plastic grape arbor. The mood on the dance floor was festive: the men yipped and waved their arms like lassos. "This is fairly hokey," I said.

"No. It's great." She was up, and started to do all the kick-scoot moves; she didn't have belt loops to put her thumbs through, so she was pressing down the bell of her dress, and it puffed out behind. She clapped. It killed me that she was so adaptable. The whole rank rolled its shoulders at once, pivoted, and clapped. Some of the cowboys looked gentle and downcast, concentrating on their moves. Some were on parade. A lesser girl might have beamed, starstruck, at the men, but Adrienne was so clearly aristocratic—she simply knew how to behave. When I downed my drink (it was blue) and finally strode onto the floor she made room for me, but that was it. She was busy with heel work. I tried to glide, tap, and twirl. I thought about Chase: Was she cheating on him? Were we here because she was hiding from him? Was this being discreet? Or was it flagrant? Or was it maybe from me that she was hiding? We were the only straight couple here.

Such self-discipline was new to me: Keeping my elbows in, clapping, watching where I stepped. Whirling in a circumscribed place. I took a lesson from the men I watched. For them, the exercise in self-control meant something. They looked careworn, mild, like men who had had a bad week. It was nothing now to behave.

Among them Adrienne was formidable. She was a woman. She had an imperturbable face. The down on her arms flashed in the light. After the line dance broke up she bought off the regulars snapping her fingers, winking at them (or laughing), doing all these flourishes, and I tried to match, I would keep my wrist behind my back or something, like a matador, and set my face. And then I would go crazy. One man wagged his finger at me and shouted, I'm sure I misheard: "Tongue *out*."

Afterwards, we went to a gas station for coffee. I can still see Adrienne in heels, bearing our coffees back under the gas station lights—the cube of light made by the Texaco canopy. I had parked with our back to the highway's sound barrier, and Adrienne's heels echoed like in an empty auditorium. I smiled from behind my windshield, and Adrienne smiled back. She had a coffee in each hand.

We sat parked in the car, facing the station. On the highway behind us we heard the rigs whining, each one like it was about to slam into us, coming at a high pitch, and then muttering off into the night. That went on the whole time we sat there. "He's waiting for us to make out," Adrienne said. The station attendant, trapped in his control booth with the lottery telemetry, was staring at us. He wondered if we were Bonnie and Clyde, come to kill him.

I cleared my throat. "*Aren't* we going to make out?"

Adrienne looked at me. Then she said, "You get points for that." She lunged for her purse. "Can I smoke in here?"

She had depressed my car's cigarette lighter, and now it popped.

"Wait, can I see that?" I had to wait for her to get her cigarette burning, and then she handed it over. The lighter's coils were glowing orange. "I never knew how these worked before."

"Do you want a cigarette?"

"No."

She lit one for me.

I tried to give it back.

"It's already lit. You have to smoke it."

I held the cigarette out the window, but stopped short of throwing it away. There were those warnings, I knew, posted by gas pumps.

"I thought they weighed more than this," I said. I waved my cigarette around in the air, light as a butterfly.

"Hrmf. You're too good for me Jim."

She sucked on her cigarette, apparently thinking. I leveraged over on the emergency brake and kissed her.

She had moved her cigarette out of the way—but she made it a short kiss, and I had to sit back down on my side of the car.

"You could find a better girl than me Jim."

I peered back. "You don't even know me."

"I know myself. I'm *old*." She sniggered and drew her cigarette to her mouth.

"We're the same age."

"Yes, but—" And here she made a self-upwelling gesture.

I was sitting with my armpit clamped over the steering wheel, regarding her. "You know—part of what I like about you is the possibility that you actually are this arrogant."

"Oh," she said, "yeah." She shivered. "I wish I was."

"You are."

"Jim—you know I don't go to school?"

"What do you mean?"

"Like I'm not going. Some people never go to college. Are you shocked? You're shocked."

"No, no—I'm not. Did you not get in?"

"Oh, wow. You get points for that too."

"With your art and with this—the way you have—you could write an *amazing* essay—"

Adrienne had never even finished high school. "When I turned sixteen I went to the guidance counselor and said, 'I want to drop out now.' And the counselor looked at me and said, 'Are you asking me to talk you out of it?' And I was like, 'No, I just want to do it right.' And the counselor was like, 'You just stop coming.' So I did. The only person who even tried to stop me was Chase. Whom you know?"

"Yeah—yes. But you just said *whom*. I don't know, in a weird way I think all that would impress colleges—your just doing that, as if you've had this plan all along. Outside the box. It's ruthless. And that you've actually done something with your time."

She was annoyed.

"You do things," I said.

"You haven't seen those things."

"Yes but I can tell that you are for real."

"Jim," she said after a minute. "Tell me a story."

"What kind of story?"

"A story that's sacred to you."

It had never occurred to me to have a story that was "sacred" to me. It was like college application essays—mine at least, which I had almost had to make up. We were asked about an experience that changed our lives. An important experience. I wrote about an epiphany I'd had while standing atop a large rock. I had stood there, and I picked up some kind of vibration about my destiny. Basically, that I realized I wanted to be a statue when I died, a great man.

"In the second grade," I began now, "we were assigned to write stories about an imaginary place. And my teacher, who still used the paddle, right, and was this very august African-American lady, sat us down in a circle. I volunteered mine for her to read, and she took it up. I was the teacher's pet. But she gave me this look. Like her jaw dropped.

"My story was about backwards-land. So naturally I titled it after my backwards-named city. Aslut. Which is Tulsa backwards."

I paused.

"But the crucial detail here is that I wasn't able to figure out what the matter with the title had been, until years later."

"Oh," said Adrienne. She gloated a little with me.

"Yeah."

Adrienne was going to tell me one. First, five seconds to collect herself: she had obviously told this story before, but maybe not often. She related it in hushed tones, and paused often—as if it really was sacred. It was like she regarded her younger self as a more important, more trustworthy person than her present self.

"There was a fifth-grader named Derek Walkin. He was bringing a Zippo to school, and that was a big deal. They would set trash on fire behind the dumpster. And they let me watch. I was little. I was a second-grader. Every day at lunch I would go up to their group and stand there. I thought they would kick me out. But I didn't even look at them—their faces. I just stared at the fire.

"But. I wanted the lighter. I searched Derek's locker. But he always kept it in his pocket." Adrienne was staring straight ahead, as if she could still see the little Zippo working on the playground. "I went up to him and asked him for it. I wanted to borrow it. Which was madness." Adrienne's voice turned excitable. "I don't know if you know what it takes, for a second-grade girl to convince a fifth-grade boy to give her *his lighter*? I caught him alone after school and at first just asked him to show me how it worked. It always looked like he was doing something weird with his wrist, shaking it or something—you've seen Zippos. You have to do like that—" She motioned. "I thought I had to get it right the first time or he would never let me borrow it. But my hands were so little."

"What happened?"

"It took me like eight tries."

"What did he say?"

Adrienne squinted. "He just let me borrow it."

"Wow. Why?"

"I don't know. He just did. He wasn't a very well-liked boy."

I could imagine a boy like that. A semi passed behind us, rattling. Adrienne was so acute, so practical in her dealings. It was quiet at the gas station, there wasn't even canned music. Adrienne resumed. "He gave me his lighter because I told him what I was going to do with it. In fact the main reason he almost didn't give it to me was that he got scared. I made him prove he wasn't.

"I took that lighter that weekend and I set fire to my aunt's garage. I burned it down to the ground."

"Oh."

Adrienne blinked. "For a while the fire was kind of nice. It spread out like at the bottom part of the wall. I stayed inside with it, to feed it, and pulled down rags and pieces of wood to keep it going. It took forever. But then it got big fast." Adrienne widened her eyes. "What I hadn't expected was how loud it would be. I had gone to stand by my favorite tree, to watch. For a long time I could hear the fire more than see it. I could see smoke, but that was all. Until the flames burst out the window.

They broke the glass like a fist." She pumped her fist, but slowly. "I had a cordless phone too, in my hand, to call 911 if the fire spread. And I wanted to call, you know. I wanted them to stop it. But I had to stick to my plan. I had to watch that garage burn down to the ground. It was mine; I was only seven years old but I *knew*, I knew then, that nothing was ever going to feel that big again." She looked at me appraisingly. "I've always wanted to get that feeling back again."

I wasn't supposed to speak, and didn't speak. As she waited she raised her hand, hung it in the air, and let it drop and crumple in her lap.

"That thing I made you," I said.

She raised her eyebrows. "I liked it."

I felt like I had taken a nap and woken up: I could sit in that car forever. "Look. That story. Write down what you just said and that's your essay."

Adrienne did want me to tell her about college. And she acted like I knew more about college, or had more quintessentially been to college, than the kids who went in-state. She was adroit, and at some level she was playing me. But at another level Adrienne was quite sincere. In fact no one had been so thorough, trying to form a picture of what I had learned.

Adrienne asked what did my classes have to do with my *work*—I had told her about a poem I was writing, called "Outskirts," which was going to be very long and which transposed the city limits of Tulsa to a number of different locales—Tulsa as an oil emirate, Tulsa as an island in the South Pacific, Tulsa as a suburb of New York.

"But I'm not really taking each class except on hunches; it's like choosing a book to read I guess, it's going to be background information down the road."

Adrienne understood me, but her own curiosity was more urgent. She wanted to know specifically about my art history course. "You should teach me," she said.

This was something I could do. Immediately I brought in all the boring logistics: I had left my textbooks at school, in storage, but I eagerly outlined how I could pull relevant books at the library and bring them to her, and we could go over them.

"Let's do it tomorrow," she said. And she put on her seat belt.

"I thought you were trying to get rid of me."

"No you didn't. You're a better listener than that Jim."

Every morning at eight I would nose my car down into the Booker's garage. I pretended I had gotten a job there, that I worked for Booker Petroleum. Men not much older than me waited in shirts and ties for the elevator, while I took the brass bench in the lobby and sat with my art books on my lap—those books were too big to hide, so I decided to be rather brazen. I had Old Master nudes and just sat there with my elbows on my knees, looking at the pictures. I sucked on my iced coffee until Adrienne came down.

She was calling me at six, six-thirty to wake me up. "Routine is an art," she informed me.

This went on for about two weeks.

On exceptional mornings, calling at six, she told me not to come. "I'm seeing something; I'm going to go on over and get started."

"Okay." I would make some excuse to my parents and go back to bed.

But most mornings, Adrienne put on one of her bright skirts and her heels and came down to meet me—she took these rush-hour walks like a morning constitutional. We traveled every morning through the streets of downtown, across the tracks, to the old brick loft where she worked. It was a little over a half mile's distance—all within the bounds of the inner dispersal loop. It was good to be a pedestrian. Adrienne had a small Japanese motorcycle in the Booker garage, but she seldom used it. "I don't have a car," she said. "I don't want a car."

That first day when we got to the studio I tromped upstairs, iced coffee in hand, ready to emote and discuss. But I didn't yet realize what my role was. When we got to the top of the stairs Adrienne put her finger to her lips and led me into a darkness. At the far end of the space, with a giant iron screeching, she yanked back the big industrial shutters—and in the flood of milky light I saw her already opening her paints, no longer making eye contact with me, and I was uncertain, and I sat down.

Instead of showing me her paintings, Adrienne simply started to work. I didn't know what I had thought was going to happen, but I was shocked that she could think while I sat there watching. She lifted her brush and made a stroke. It paralyzed me. I could see several of her canvases from my couch—they looked like the real thing. They were big abstract shapes, and the canvases were huge.

Only when she wanted a break did she turn to me, and then not to chat or heaven forbid touch or kiss, but to go through the art books. I prepped each night, giving her my art history course as I remembered it and going artist by artist. I was half diffident at first, irritated at the paused status of my love suit, I didn't expect Adrienne to like artists like Greuze or Chardin. Both made plain, watered-down pictures, people dying, people in wigs bending over to pick a spoon off the floor, or a mother sitting at a wooden kitchen table with her children. Chardin she might like, if at all, because this young wife resembled her, painted with the white neck and the tapering, pinkened fingers. In fact every night, in the air-conditioned parental house when my parents had gone to bed and I sat with a heavy art book in my lap, I thought of Adrienne most bodily, much more so than when I was in her studio. I fantasized about us actually being at college together: we strayed into my dorm room together, after the art lecture.

Adrienne was an even better student than I had intuited. Her exposure as a child to her aunt's milieu—not just an arsonist at seven, but equally the child at the table at dinner and at parties—served Adrienne better than she knew. And she had a work ethic. She had taught herself to be extremely patient. "I used to be in rock bands," she told me, "except I wanted to rehearse so much nobody would work with me." While looking at the art books she always wanted to stop and spend five minutes with her nose in a picture, in silence. And this

53

would be longer than I had spent on it. "You're wrong about Chardin," she said one day. "He's so mellow. His color is perfect."

"That chair is the same color as that piece of meat," I put in.

It could be Adrienne was putting up a front, to show that going to college had nothing to do with painterly knowledge. She knew that her lack of education could hurt her—if she failed in life, people would say so. Her aunt would certainly say so. Perhaps I, with my alma mater, represented her aunt, and Adrienne wanted to school me. But Adrienne's eyes when she looked at the pictures were honest. And she did seem to take a personal interest in me. Otherwise I wouldn't have kept coming. Though Adrienne did not once that week directly ask me how I liked her paintings. What compliments I offered weren't listened to. And there was no touching, no kissing.

"What does Chase have that I don't?" I once asked her.

"You're happy, Jim."

"What?"

"You're the only person I've ever liked who's so happy."

I always took a nap as soon as we got to the studio: I wasn't used to early mornings. I lowered myself down by my stomach muscles, very gradually; I always tried to angle my head in such a way that Adrienne might want to come over and inspect me, my head and my neck, my ear, or my arm. I respected her strictures and her sense that the studio was a sacred place, but I assumed she would break her rules, when the climax came. It didn't.

She addressed her easel and I addressed my notebook. When I couldn't think of the next line to write, I could look over and watch her paint. She wore overalls to paint, usually. She could stand in front of the easel for five minutes without doing anything, and I watched. When she felt like it Adrienne might say something offhand—but it had to be poised, our talk, talk that could stop on a dime. She raised her brush again, and I shut up.

My parents didn't know why I was waking up so early. I was quick at breakfast, silent, going over what I would say about that day's artist. Overall I loved it. After years of staring at downtown, my perspective revolved in. Adrienne pulled the city inside out for me: she chose the most built-up streets for our morning walks—for a block or two we existed in an urban canyon; had we gone the opposite way, the horizon would have emptied out, the skyscrapers would have given out on limp down-tempo parking lots and strip malls. But for a block, I at least could imagine that we had been born in a bigger city. I loved to talk about that, alternate destinies and fate. I liked to pretend it was very strange to have been born in a place like Tulsa.

I tried to be open; I tried to tell Adrienne about the things I liked. That on First Street in the mornings the concrete turns to gray putty. That in a state of grace you could imagine the concrete lines going on straight forever. But of course the skyscrapers crest, Tulsa buckles, the cross streets slope up; they have to span over the tracks.

Adrienne introduced me to the eight a.m. rush hour that fleetingly brings downtown to life: she wore heels mainly out of respect for her family—to look decent in the Booker Petroleum elevator but also out of respect for the brief daily flowering of downtown Tulsa. That there were people in suits, people who parked and got out of their cars and massed at the crosswalks as people in a big-city movie might. It lasted all of ten minutes, commencing at eightish and then again at five. But seeing it did more for my sense of downtown than twenty years of downtown church had.

Of course, Adrienne wasn't preoccupied by such things. We passed by the Episcopal church, and she merely said, "It's nice." We passed by the Performing Arts Center, and she said, "It's an eyesore." The ingrained culture war, the knee-jerk resentment·that most kids have for the conservative town, didn't seem to worry her. She never had any problem going to Wal-Mart, she simply loved that she could buy things, and ran circles around her cronies. "That flag," I said, pointing to one in the sporting goods section that had slipped partway off the wall, "they're supposed to burn it. That's what you're technically supposed to do, when they touch the ground. Burning flags is actually extremely patriotic." Adrienne didn't care.

And she never swore. "Downtown is so fucking lively," I said, and immediately noticed how crass it sounded—I got frustrated sometimes. Sometimes I wanted to throw my old life against Adrienne. There was a man with a jeep who was always parallel-parking between Second and Third, I recognized him through his windshield two days in a row. "I think that guy was my Sunday school teacher," I told Adrienne.

I kept mentioning Sunday school and church. Adrienne

had been in choir at First Presbyterian and had liked it. "But you didn't have to go," I said, "every seventh morning of adolescence—they asked us to sign a pledge card once, pledging never to have premarital sex. They told us that people regret premarital sex for the rest of their lives."

"Maybe it's true."

"They actually said, 'When you get married you will stand at the altar with your bride and, in, like, a nightmare, see all the other women you've ever slept with, all lined up, holding hands with your bride, grinning at you.' It was obscene."

"Don't act outraged," she said. "You're not convincing as an outraged person."

"What do you think he thinks of us though? In the jeep. Surely he doesn't look at us and say, There go two young coworkers, on their way to the office."

"Do you care? I thought you hated Sunday school."

"No," I stressed. "Him—I crave his respect."

One morning, when the man from the jeep was about to pass, I stopped him. "Mr. Bangs?"

He was heavier than I remembered, his face flecked with salmon, blurred. I introduced myself. "Jim Praley. I was in your Sunday school class. You were the small group leader, and we used to go into the little room."

He was solicitous—he thought he had to reprise his mentoring role. I told him I was a college sophomore in the fall, we always walked this way to my friend Adrienne's studio, to paint.

"This is my friend Adrienne Booker," I said.

"Okay, I believe I work for your aunt, Ms. Booker."

Adrienne smiled and nodded very graciously.

He leaned over a bit as he shook our hands goodbye, his tie hanging plumb.

We ranged over the sidewalk going on. Adrienne was silent, and I was obscurely apprehensive. I dashed ahead of her and balanced atop a fire hydrant. At the corner of First and Main the Performing Arts Center's big digital sign, with its scramble of lightbulbs bringing off a firework, exploded, showed the temperature Fahrenheit, and then admitted that *La Bohème* was in town, boom boom boom, as if anybody cared.

"Was that rude? Of me to introduce you like that?"

"Why?"

"I don't know. That we're just betaking ourselves off to our artistic pursuits? And—mentioning your last name."

"Is that something you think is important?"

I trailed her the rest of the way, down First, across the tracks, and then down among the warehouses of the Brady District.

Later that day, I realized she wasn't working. I woke from my nap and lay, as was my habit, in the depression my body had made. Usually this was the most private part of my day—when our mutual silence was as constructive for me as it was for her. But today I couldn't think, an aggravated silence ballooned in my head the instant I realized I was awake. I endured it for a short while, and then got up and rinsed my mouth. Adrienne was standing in front of her easel, hands behind her back, staring at me. I said I would go out and get our lunches. When I got back I was glad to see her bent over a tall table—one she rarely used—apparently drawing. I set her lunch down at her elbow, and then went and took up my writing pad. We ate our lunches in nutritious silence.

I wrote on. My pen-scratching was the only sound in the room, but I didn't care if it annoyed her. When I heard footsteps coming around behind me, I didn't turn. I saw her raising up her leg like an equestrienne. She straddled my belt and undid my shirt. "Lie back," she whispered, "I'm going to draw on you." Her marker was large and black. The ink felt refreshing at first, wet. But I was not proud of my chest: the way she sat on me, studying me, for minutes at a time between marks. Mainly I was having a transport of obedience. "This is so nerve-wracking," she said, bearing down on me. She would close one eye, spread my skin with two fingers, and mark. Just an inch or two, or once (the process had grown excruciating) an endless black wing, like cold water, flowing across my nipple. It went like that, her leaning back and me supine: me an artwork, with my chest hairs.

After she was done, she stood me up in front of the mirror: I had an embellished arabesque glyph on my chest, large and highly visible, the kind of thing that as graffiti would make you stop and look. She really was talented.

"To do that on someone," she said, "I think you have to really like them."

She meant the tension in the act of drawing: that she could bring it off while concentrating atop me. It proved that she liked me?

Later that day, she broke down. We were looking at

another one of my library books: *The Passion of Dela-croix.*

"This has nothing to do with anything," she said. Her eyes were wet.

"It's just Delacroix."

"No it's, what did you say—"

"Trivial?"

"It's trivial."

"But what we're doing—it's not." I said.

"Why do you not think so?"

"Do you feel trivial right now?"

"No."

"Well."

She blinked. "But I'm not working. I've been spending too much time with these books."

"I won't bring them tomorrow."

"Jim. I should go back to painting alone."

"Okay."

"I'm afraid I've been missing something," she said.

And then I started sleeping in again. I went to the Blumont that weekend and got drunk alone. I went walking, and ended up underneath the clinking flagpole at the Center of the Universe, where I found encampments of all types of white kids smoking pot, telling legends under the June night about Hitler, and Wu-Tang, and the CIA. Nobody offered me anything, to partake or to buy. I thought I recognized a few faces, maybe just types. Anyway, I was too nervous, and walked back to my car with my hands in my pockets.

I had lost control of the summer. I had interrupted

my self-imposed study program to pursue Adrienne, and now all my dreams and random thoughts went feeling towards her. I sprawled on my parents' carpet and thought about the cool poured concrete of the studio.

"I'm painting," she said.

"I can call back later." My heart raced, just to have her on the line.

"I painted something I will want to show you."

"I can come over now—"

"No—I have to figure some things out, Jim."

"I was going to ask you to go to Stars again." I cast my eyes down. I had asked.

"I've got to wait a minute. I'll call you later this week."

"Should I—"

"No."

I sank to my knees. The blood had gone out of my head, and I needed to lay my face in the carpet to rest.

4

I heard through Edith: Adrienne had invited me to come
on a weekend to Bartlesville. What Adrienne imagined
this would be like is, in retrospect, unclear. Edith called
up out of the blue, chiding me for neglect, for spending
all my time with Adrienne only—when I hadn't seen
Adrienne in a week. "She said maybe you could give me
and Cam a ride to Bartlesville." I pretended I knew what
Bartlesville meant: beyond that it was a small city thirty
minutes to the north, the home of Phillips Petroleum.
I packed a shirt and tie, my sleeping bag, and even a
swimsuit.

Bartlesville meant Albert Dooney's cabin. His family,
like so many of Oklahoma's smaller oil families in the
1920s, had built vacation homes in the long-backed hills
of Osage County. We were actually ten minutes west of
Bartlesville itself, by the shores of a tiny lake. Albert had
added a small recording studio to the fishing getaway
his grandfather had built, and he regularly invited Chase's

friends to come out for a weekend, to record. Albert was the type of man who in middle age finds comfort in the young and is happy to live with their bluster and their self-pity, the kind of man who feels fulfilled reaching his finger out, from time to time, to correct them.

Driving up, with Edith explaining some of this to me and Cam smoking and the radio on, we decided to take surface roads—I was in no hurry to arrive. The landscape reminded me of my Boy Scout excursions, a blanched summer forest up close, overgrown over miles and miles of tumbledown wire fencing. We stopped at a gas station that I even thought I remembered: the parakeets the owner kept out by the pumps. One bought beer now, instead of candy, and I traveled not with a vanload of adolescent boys but with two girls. Even better that they were lesbians.

And then we had to arrive. I always hate it when the engine switches off and you have to find yourself where you actually are, bereft of the enveloping hum of an automobile. We had been playing a complicated form of twenty questions. The designated letter was L: "Are you Michael Jackson's alleged long-distance girlfriend?" Cam asked. I had to think. "No, I am not Lisa Marie Presley." "Did you play Romeo opposite Claire Danes?" But I refused to continue, now that we had stepped out of the car.

Albert's lake house was drab, made out of brown shingles, a big saltbox with squat four-pane windows on the second floor. We walked past an ashy grill and entered through the kitchen. Our host was just sitting there, like a circus bear at a tea party. Girls were sitting at his table sorting beans, one of them on the cordless to people who hadn't left Tulsa yet, demanding that they bring this and that. Albert looked unconcerned. His eyes filled up his glasses, and he blinked thoughtfully; his limp fringe of hair lay on his collar as he turned about. "Here's the girl from Hartford," he said. I carried the beer we had brought, in cases with the cardboard finger slits turning my knuckles white—I didn't know where to set them down. Having stood with a sweet grin on my face at first, but hating the thought of being the center of attention—being introduced in a round—I plunged forward with my beers. Conscious that although Adrienne had invited me, she wasn't here yet. These others didn't know me. I rummaged around in the refrigerator, trying to make room for my beer among all the ground beef. But at the sink a boy with sandy hair and Lennon spectacles stood scouring the removable grill part of the grill, and he leaned over to see what I was doing. He told me beers went in the pantry. Where indeed I found an icebox filled with brightly colored, stackable cases of beer.

When I came back from the bathroom, Adrienne was there. She flashed me a quick lascivious smile. It said to me: Stay away. She was helping Chase get ready to grill; she was making patties for him—and, because of the meat on her hands presumably, she could not come directly to greet me. So I stepped down into the den.

This was her world then. A lot of the kids were already drunk. They were nice kids, not cutthroats, but I couldn't sit down in their badinage. They were filling up the pseudo-rustic den with dirty jokes. Had they been worthy of Adrienne, had they presented a gradual declension from her awesomeness, plateauing at a still-competent level, I would have sat down in their company and listened. But they were talking about drawing dicks on each other's faces. Of course, this was where their authority came from: being like this with each other, being paid up in full in some psychic way. It made me crazy. And it had nothing to do with membership: Cam, arguably a greater outsider than me, was sitting there talking their language. It was inevitable that I, instead, would take up position at the window, and notice how dour the conifers looked outside. I went into the next room and watched TV.

Later, I was probably the only person still indoors; I was watching the Tulsa local news when Adrienne came in and switched off the TV.

She had a younger girl in tow. "Have you met Jenny?"

I had not.

"You guys both write poetry."

I looked helplessly at Adrienne—who was already leaving. Chase was setting up his briquettes outside. I should have been furious. Jenny was obviously cute. She was a foot shorter than me and had bright, slow-moving eyes.

"You just met Adrienne?" Jenny asked.

"Um, I go watch her paint sometimes. We're going through an art history course that I give her with different books—"

"Oh my god. Her paintings are so good."

I shrugged. "They're very postwar, which I like."

Her eyes lit up. "They're totally postwar."

"I mean, if she ever really gets an idea it could be interesting."

Jenny looked hurt, but she nodded.

"Where are you in school?" I asked her. I thought I was trying to be nice, but I wasn't.

"I'm going to Union upper next year."

Something in me was on the point of snapping. "Sorry," I said. "I'll definitely see you later."

I went striding through the woods, trying to rush the gullies and boulders with old hiker's footwork, and hurried. The forest was getting dark. Only continuing on because of an obscure claim to self-righteousness, I felt sick. I couldn't stop chewing on this feeling that I had blundered. Night turned black. So I had to turn around, poking in the dark with my little key chain LED, dreading the slush of leaves beneath each footfall. I almost prayed to God with relief when I finally came back and saw the lights of a house and, untangling myself from the branches, could confirm it was Albert's.

I found some chicken on the grill, cold, wrapped in foil. I ate it with my fingers, and sat on the porch, staring into the woods. I wished I could just sit and guard the house, like a dog.

Finally I went in.

There were shapes up in the living room, dancers, trying to make a night of it. Edith sat in the kitchen, part of a big card game. I went in and got a glass of whiskey, but made eye contact with no one.

Later, having curled up under a desk in some upstairs storage room, I woke. I heard voices from below. So people were still awake. I had been drooling, and fronds of acrylic carpet were sticking to my lips. I rose, and veered out into the hall.

I met Jenny on the staircase, and we abruptly sat down. As if we had planned to meet. Jenny sat on a step below me and I started to tell her about the banister: turned wood uprights carved into the shape of pine-apples, and beneath the pineapples some other kind of wooden flourishment. She was really paying attention. The only way I could explain it to her, I said, was the way toy soldiers would use the banister to convey themselves down if they were invading the ground floor, swinging from pineapple to pineapple with grappling hook and line. Sometimes, alas, plummeting away to the soft carpet below. Poof. And then silence. Jenny gripped my knee. Then we opened our mouths partway, lined up, and kissed.

I was screwed around like a bird, to kiss her; despite the terrible sleep-taste in my mouth she was locked on me; she took my face in her hands and immediately scooted up to my step, quite competent. At least it's some-thing that's happened, I said to myself. It was Jenny who stood us up, and suggested we go out and watch the sun rise. As we flew out the door I plucked a bottle of gin off the table, and she swept up an afghan on top her head. It felt like the sky was lightening faster than we could cross the yard.

The next night was similar. After a dull day of campfire chatter, and the ceaseless back-and-forth of new people up from town, band people off to the studio, and after the much-hyped assembly of turducken, I was fading into the background, having drunk all afternoon; I found myself heading upstairs again, taking the stairs in giant steps, slowly, wobbling, turning into the same storage room, and curling up for a nap just the same, shortly after dark. I slept for a long time. And when I woke up, deep in the night, with the carpet imprinted on the side of my face, it felt like time had looped, and I resolved to myself to do something good with my life, to break the loop.

I didn't go down the stairs this time but continued around the landing, and careened truly innocently into a bedroom where the light was on. Beneath the light, Adrienne and Chase lay there sleeping. They were strewn on the bed below me, covered with blankets. I was riveted. I stood there with a rocky feeling on my face. I stood and studied Adrienne's nose, pressed flat on its side, an intense rose color smushed on the white pillowcase. Adrienne cracked an eye.

But it was Chase who got it together and unfurled an arm to greet me. "Join us," he said, his voice hoarse.

I didn't believe it.

"Come on," said Chase. "Come get some sleep?"

They weren't touching; they were sleeping in different halves of the bed. I stepped out of my shoes.

To climb in, I had to plant my knee and hand beside Chase. Then I hesitated. "Should I turn out the light?"

Chase smiled, amused. "Yes."

Then I made my way back to the bed and, planting a knee without touching Chase, I tried to bridge across them to get down on the far side of Adrienne. She rolled away, however. And then Chase just pulled me down like a dog. He laid his arm across me. "It's cool," he said.

He fumbled with the sheets, and I helped him. We were all three tucked in now. I didn't know whether either of them had pants on, or were naked below the waist. "Time to sleep," Chase said. I squirmed so as to be faceup, neither ass nor lips toward Chase—but I could already hear his even breathing.

From Adrienne's direction, silence. To be in the same warm bed with her was like a lightbulb turned on in my belly. I lay there, waiting to see if her leg would move. I waited for what seemed like hours, to see if she would touch me, afraid all the time on the other side that Chase would stir. Chase was a bear. He would roll over on me without differentiating. From Adrienne's side I waited for a sign. I inched my leg nearer her, but was nowhere near touching. I had no idea how long it was, my eyes had adjusted, when I finally turned on my side to look at her. Her face was sleeping. The emotion that usually held her face was gone. I raised my head so I could look at her ear—her head looked like it was carved out of soap. Her nose was softer than usual, her cheeks more substantial. Her open mouth was the only thing that was completely dark. I stared, and made my body quiet. Adrienne would have wanted me to control myself. I slept, but it was sleep like in airports, waiting. I saw her sometimes. I opened my eyes and she rolled away, but when hours—maybe minutes—had passed, she rolled back, and I kissed her. She opened her eyes to acknowledge it and moved her sleepy arms to pull me closer. I kept my eyes open too. The kissing was perfect, slick, and noisy. Adrienne got on top of me, and pushed my hair back, and pressed her thumbs to my temples as if it was her

70

own forehead she was trying to clear, to keep from going crazy. She looked down at me—I thought it was the long look of someone completing their love, but of course Chase had woken up, and Adrienne was only looking to see if I was okay, before she moved. After crawling over, she sat on his stomach as she had sat on mine—it was like she was harvesting something from him, the way she kissed him, with her eyes closed, rutting her chin forward and back. His eyes slid open and he looked at me, unmistakably amused. It was not unfriendly though. The sun was coming up and we were beginning to be able to see better. I was completely out of time. If I felt jealous, I was not anguished. More than anything I was eager. I was rapt, until Chase put his hand out to me. We held hands, like people about to fall off the bed. He kind of gripped to give me strength. And then Adrienne disengaged, and got off him, and squatted at the foot of the bed. Nothing happened. We heard stirrings from the floor below. Inspired beyond reason, I dragged myself on my elbows over to Chase, and kissed him as Adrienne had. I took both of his shoulders with my hands. His tongue was rough, his teeth larger than any girl's. He was responding—I had been dared to do this. I let him rear up sort of, onto his elbow, so we posed as equals, but it was an uncomfortable angle for my neck. I had never been very good making friends with boys. Here was a great bastard. I hugged Chase, and pushed him back down, and looked at him. He was ugly. His blond eyelashes were stubby, his eyelids wrinkled. He grunted and moved away. Then Adrienne embraced me from behind, and kissed me inside my ear. It was not sweet, it was not straightforward. I wanted to wriggle away so I could face her—but I didn't. Adrienne clamped her arm across my breast. "The it-boy," said Chase, looking at me. He was grinning hugely. We were all, absurdly now, waddling on our knees—there was more stirring from belowstairs—I worried my face would give away all my thoughts. Chase leaned in for more kissing. Adrienne held me. My heart was racing. Finally he stopped. Adrienne had let go. I lumbered around and looked at her. Her face was blank. I was in there now, I kissed her. Our lips were soft this time, and quiet. Each other's faces felt composed. We breathed louder. Her cheek was inside my neck, her nose was inside my eye, and I breathed and mutely talked to her. "I'm going to take a shower," we heard Chase say. We heard the water from the adjoining bathroom. Adrienne pushed down my pants with her thumbs. She got back under the covers and I followed. She pulled the blankets over us. I thought she would look at me intensely; I thought she would still be deciding, while I was inside her, whether she wanted this. But it wasn't like that at all. She edged her chin back, gasping. Her throat worked, and her teeth showed, eyes wide open and straining at the headboard. Like she was biting a stream of ice. Then she moaned, so Chase could hear. I could not believe how okay I was in this situation. Her eyes tilted into her forehead. With the blankets over us I felt that we had moved into a tent and were going to live in it together. When she finally looked at me I came. Her look was calm, accepting, betrothal-like. With her arm crooked over my head I didn't have anything to give her, so I worked both arms beneath her and squeezed, but that felt insincere. Chase was going to come out of the bathroom and see us—but Chase was not going to care, and that was the lesson. She slid her leg over me. She was hot. I worked myself up so that I could penetrate her again. This time was not so urgent, and it was not so honest, it was a little violent, it was in large part to cover for ourselves for when Chase came out, so that he could not interrupt us, so that he would have to shut up. But it was going even better mechanically than before. Adrienne was sweating. When I heard the bathroom door open I stopped, but she kept moving, and I felt like a hog. I glanced, looking for Chase. He was somewhere behind me, getting dressed. He didn't hurry or anything. Adrienne had stopped too. My face was planted in the pillow. The only movement in the room was him getting dressed. Then he left and we resumed (nothing felt better); we could hear him jogging downstairs.

We slept. A bit later, the sun already high, our bedroom—somebody's bedroom, Albert's guest bedroom—was warm. I plowed my hands into the empty regions of the sheets to feel their coolness. Adrienne turned over. We probably stank, we had already stunk of sleep when we started. We would be craving showers. I laid my nostrils on Adrienne's arm, in the crook of her elbow. She smelled like a Band-Aid. The skin pressed the rims of my nostrils. I didn't quite have rights to her body yet: she stirred, and I drew back. She opened her lazy eyes onto me, and didn't move or avert them: it was the most intimate thing. I wanted to have some cynical remark, about layabouts, about exhaustion, but affection overwhelmed me. Her gaze persisted, staring, I shambled onto her, dazed, locked in this time, sweating.

At noon, again, on purpose. With empty bellies, with an inexplicable hoarse feeling in our throats. In full color. Like an apology to the people downstairs. The cords of her throat straining red, like it wasn't fun. But I did not let her get out into the clean air. I held her in the burning sheets. We fell asleep with all our skin touching, just to make the heat worse, to sweat more.

Much later, Chase poked his head in. "Um, people are leaving."

Adrienne ripped off a sheet, flipped it in her arms once, and then drew it over her head, hunching like a crone. She was going to go home with Chase, of course. "I must cover zee head," she said, "for modestee."

As I was loading Edith and Cam's stuff back into my car, Chase came up and punched me in the gut. He was friendly, grinding his fist in my belly. "Okay," he said, looking appraising, ironic: he approved. He waved good-bye as Edith and Cam and I drove off.

"You should be nice to Chase," said Edith. Our windows were still down; we had not yet left the property. The soft tinkle of tires on gravel was all our tired ears wanted to hear.

"Why?"

"You're not in competition with him."

"How do you know?"

"They've never been like boyfriend and girlfriend. They're like siblings."

"I'm not so sure about that," I said.

We got onto the main road and we rolled up our windows. Edith rode in silence for a while. "You know Jim, Adrienne grew up really unsupervised. Eventually she started dating guys in bands. It got pretty intense. They heard her sing and . . . have you heard her sing? She was fourteen. There were all these guys. Without Chase she never would ever have survived."

"You mean literally survived?" I asked.

"Yeah. Maybe not, Jim."

The late-afternoon sun glared in my windshield. It was dirty. I wondered if it would seem passive-aggressive if I stopped at a gas station to wash it. I felt irritated: I should have had that drive home to myself.

Edith had said: "Adrienne and Chase were little kids together, their families were friends. I don't know how gradual it was, but he just started being there for her. And no matter who she was seeing she always had Chase. He gave her a lot of stability."

"You mean she slept with him and other men too?"

"I guess!"

"And so I can be a new version of those other men."

My parents complained about the cigarette smell in my car. They had not driven it since I came home. I arrived back from Bartlesville however and fell asleep, and that was when my dad took it upon himself to get my oil changed.

"I guess because people don't roll their windows down," I said.

This took place not at the dinner table, which would have been too theatrical for my parents' tastes, but cleaning up afterwards. I was carrying plates, while my dad washed the dishes. My mom took up position in the doorway and lobbed questions at me.

So who were these friends, that I let them smoke in my car?

It didn't seem necessary that I should name them. "People," I said. "I don't know. Are you worried about secondhand smoke?" But that obviously wasn't the point, any more than olfactory contamination was the point. My mom persisted. "Look," I said. I took up the chopping knife and the cutting board. "My friends smoke. So I let them smoke in my car."

"But how do you know they're your friends?"

I looked at her. She had gone too far. And she knew it. "By looking at their art," I said. "I know them by their works."

I was trying to pretend to be exasperated. But my Bible quote was gratuitous. "I know it seems all bohemian," I said, "and therefore stupid—or stupid and unconvincing to be bohemian, maybe, in this day and age." I still tried to shrug. "I don't know, I learn more from them than I do from my professors. I guess that seems naïve."

This was the biggest fight I had had with my parents in memory. They were very quiet. My dad stood by afterwards, sort of waiting as I dried the dishes. I told him about a Kissinger book I was reading, transcripts of Kissinger's telephone conversations with Golda Meir and others from 1973. I knew it would interest him. He took up the plates to shelve them.

"I guess what I should say to Mom is something like—I won't lose track of who I am."

My father had an equilateral nose with long, wolfish

nostrils, and thin, neat lips, and it seemed to cost him nothing to process what I had said, to find a kernel of goodwill and good sense in it. I immediately regretted having said anything at all, and at the same time was helped, beyond reckoning, by my father's grace.

The day I brought Adrienne her gun—I'm still so proud of how crazy that was. I parked outside Adrienne's studio one bright July morning with a small blue pistol in my glove compartment. Which I retrieved and hefted—the way you heft any present for which you have paid too much and which, held in your own hand before you give it, trembles less with the recipient's desires than with your own.

At Adrienne's invitation I had started going to the studio again, that week after Bartlesville. But still my bid for romantic partnership went unrecognized. She did not want to do anything at night, she did not touch me, did not invite me up to the penthouse. And I made no reference to what had happened.

I had literally thought about getting Adrienne flowers. The gun was the superior idea. What thrilled me was the presumption: after all, you can't make someone own a gun. But I believed I had to presume. God stands up for the presumptuous. For me to have decided to present her with a firearm—I cannot adequately advertise how excessive this felt.

It was supposed to be obvious. At Wal-Mart, I had pushed up on tiptoe at the display counter, looking around for the clerk, worried maybe that I would flub the names and gauges I had memorized—but at least I had a show going, a blond genius with long legs and a paintbrush, and I was going to buy her a little gun for her birthday.

It was cold to the touch that next morning. This was $300; the scrollwork was cheap; the butt was long and fancy. Looking out at the empty, sunny street, the shuttered bar, the neat public trash can, I felt rebuked. I opened my car door and sat with my feet on the asphalt, trying to get the courage to go up. What had I accomplished so far that summer? I had a loaded gun in my lap, anybody walking by would have seen. But the street was dead. I think it was a Sunday—I remember the stairway up pierced with light.

Characteristically, Adrienne kept her back to me when I came in. Her smock was tied askew and I could see into her overalls where her ribs were bare. I just stood there. She inhaled and raised the paintbrush. "I have something for you," I said.

At the last second I had wrapped the gun up in a pair of jeans I found in my backseat. She pulled up at one of the pant cuffs, and the gun tumbled out.

"Did you know you can just go to the store and buy one of these things?"

She had stepped back slightly, as if from a snake.

"My god."

I had thought she would ring with laughter. But no. "It's for you," I said, swallowing my words.

She looked worried. She used her smock to pick up the gun, wielding it away from her as if she wanted to avoid fingerprints. She bent her elbow and aimed the gun at me.

"It's loaded," I told her.

She squinted, as if lining up the sight. She aimed straight at my belly.

But her voice was strained. "Why is it loaded?" she asked.

Her studio, on two sides, had windows made of glass brick. I said I wanted to shoot at the bricks, to see how they'd explode. "I didn't mean for this to seem as aggressive as it maybe does."

Not only did Adrienne inspire me, she inspired me too much: such a crazy, serious gift idea, because it was for Adrienne. Yet she proved that she deserved it. She took off the safety, lifted, turned, and aimed.

"It's going to be loud—" she said, spreading her feet apart and raising the gun. The glass bricks were full of sun.

At the instant of bullet ejection my eyes closed, like during a sneeze, but I thought I saw strands of blond hair fly back and then float down. At the back of the sound (a wide bolus of white noise), I heard a satisfying splat, and the tinkle of glass.

She fired again, almost flip.

"You?"

My ears were ringing but I took the gun. I had fired a .357 in Scouts, and had been mentally rehearsing the grip and the proper firing stance.

And I fired.

The crack was upsetting this time; it came and went not with the civilized sound of a "report" but hacked quickly at my wrists. There was a larger puff of gray— less solid than the first. I didn't know what to do next. Adrienne had taken a turn, I had taken a turn. We had deafened ourselves.

Maybe I should have shot holes through her canvases if I had brought this gun to her studio. Because she was bored already. She was edging back towards her easel. I softly laid the gun on the table, so as not to distract her.

The rest of the story is too private to make sense: Nothing happened. Adrienne got back to work. I lay down. Soon the only thing out of the ordinary was the wind that trickled in through the chinks that we'd made. Neither of us remarked on it. Neither of us felt that we should break the silence. As I was drifting off—I was abashed enough to feel a kind of pressure on my eyes, like sleepiness—I formed the improbable concern that this air from the window was going to affect her paint, dry it or sort of blow it sideways on the canvas.

It had become my habit, at the studio, to lie still for a while after naps, with the unaired taste of my own saliva still in my mouth. I did some of my longest thinking that way. It was how I had dreamed up the gun thing. I had had second thoughts, but ultimately had decided not to go back on something that had been so gleamingly intuitive.

Only now (back on the couch, after the smoke had cleared) did the intuition shine forth again, dumb and blue. I saw it for what it was: not love, but jealousy. Over that short courtship I had grown envious of this person, Adrienne, and, impatient to be like her, I had attempted this stunt. An impulse regrettably punctuated with Colt precision. Never in my mind or in any other part of my body did it occur to me to scare her, but I did want that shot, near her wrist, to put that crack in her space. I would wake from a nap and see her about to draw a line of the blackest force, her bare arm tingling above the raw canvas, studying, studying, and then taking only a simple cursive stroke, while my own arm lay buried in the couch.

I was so ardent now it felt like we were breaking up. Adrienne could see I needed to talk, and after her silent painting session ended, and with the gunshot still ringing in our ears, we decided on a five o'clock supper. I suggested the Black-Eyed Pea, a busy family-style restaurant from my childhood. As we followed the hostess to our table, I couldn't hear the hubbub so much as see it: the waiters back and forth to do refills at the soda fountain, a polished plow nailed up high on the wall.

Adrienne's luminous pointed face watched me.

"I think the gun was really an attempt to make some sort of statement," I said, while trying casually to pluck a roll from the almost-empty basket. We had left the gun in the studio; it was registered in my name, but would belong to her now. "I needed to impress you. Of course that was obvious."

"Why did you have to impress me?"

I had to lean over to be heard. "Well, I mean I was trying to speak your language." I kept glancing over behind Adrienne's shoulder, casting back to the waiting area where I used to stand when I was a twelve-year-old, in my big T-shirts, with my sandals turned out on the flagstones, waiting with my parents to be seated.

I felt desperately vague. I looked at the plow, the soda fountain, the patriotic bunting up near the ceiling. "You should be my girlfriend, Adrienne. Like boyfriend-girlfriend."

"Jim, the thing with the pistol was amazing."

"Right," I said.

"Thank you."

"But there's something more I want to talk to you about."

Her palm lay upright on the table, next to her plate; her fingers were curled up at rest, like the chicken bones. I was done apologizing that monogamy was a middle-class notion propagated by timid people—or that my people were timid, for that matter. I told her what I wanted.

"I don't have to choose like that," she said, her back up now.

"No, you're wrong," I said. She looked at me different. I had made her blink.

I licked my lips. "I think you're wrong," I continued. "You should take a boyfriend.

"I want you to date me and only me," I went on.

I sounded like the Old Testament God. And I had something very like an analogy between monotheism and monogamy in mind.

"I want to love you," I said, crossing my legs, "but, I don't know, maybe that's unwise."

Adrienne's nose broke slightly; it made her look intelligent when she glanced away.

She cracked up. "Oh!" She moaned with relish. "You're so weird!"

"I'm absolutely normal! And normative!"

"You want me to stop seeing Chase."

"And send me little cards with Valentine's Day hearts you draw on them, yes. And sleep with me."

"Don't you ever want to sleep with more than one girl?"

I rolled my eyes. "Yes but that's not the point."

"You don't know me very well."

"That's what I'm trying to say."

"Oh no you're just making fun of me."

"And yet I love you."

Adrienne was still sitting up very straight, but suddenly inhaled like she was diving underwater. And then, in the middle of the restaurant, she began to warble in my face: "GOAOD BLESS AMERRRICA, LAHND THAT I LUVV."

Her voice was preposterous, like a voluptuous brass horn curling and melting and reblowing itself before my eyes. I had to slouch back in my chair and take it. Adrienne wanted to stand up you could tell, her singing was classical, and she made those gestures you've seen, like a mime smoothing down his napkin after a meal, raising and lowering her hand at the level of her diaphragm.

She sang just that phrase, but people turned to look. There was a scattering of applause—surprised, but perfectly cheerful applause, pleased at this bel canto in our midst; people clapped. Adrienne, to my surprise, turned around and acknowledged it. Maybe that was when I knew I was going to get what I wanted.

"Was that supposed to be commentary?"

"I think it was."

"You're pretty witty for somebody who never went to college."

"Well, you inspire me Jim."

"I love you."

"That however is not true."

"It's neither untrue or true. It's an assertion I make. Same as 'fuck you.' I love you."

"Well fuck you, then."

"Should we ask for the check?"

"Yes. And then I'll take you home, and you can stay all night. How's that?"

We were very happy.

5

Adrienne allowed that Chase worked harder than I did, in bed—but she liked me too. "You're more excitable," she said.

There was a ceiling in the Booker penthouse above Adrienne's bed inlaid with zigzagged cherrywood. It was like the corners of two hundred picture frames broken apart and glued there by a man on a ladder who, in the 1920s, probably pictured a couple of fat cats for this bed. Adrienne and I were more like two sylphs, pale white fish. I got lost in that bed. I hung off the mattress, just to believe it—to look upside down out to the lip of the terrace, and there, the sky. I was surprised that houseflies came up this high—I was foremost impressed with the grandeur of the penthouse, modern with a built-in oak refrigerator and panorama windows, though on my first visits I didn't get to inspect it much, just glimpsed aerial Tulsa out the windows before Adrienne dragged me down onto the floor. The walls were forest green. When the elevator first opened you had to look at an oil painting, a horse naked except for its tail wrap. On the entry table beneath it Adrienne had put a bottle of hand lotion. And out of a double-wide beaux arts battle-ax of a wardrobe spilled garbage bags of thrift store treasure, pointy green collars and ruched whorehouse silks and gold lamé belts and slippery polyester pants.

We went up to the penthouse primarily for sex. Adrienne recommended the external-release method, which was strange, because at Bartlesville she had not cared. I complied, of course. It was tricky: I don't think Adrienne worried much about the rugs, for example, but I did, and I always reached quickly for my own underpants or for a towel—I would avoid the bed totally. I saw her bare bottom on the excellent whitework bedspread and anxiously coaxed her off of it. "I do live here, you know," she reminded me.

But Adrienne had taken my request for monogamy seriously. Sometimes she just lay back and looked at me, to see what I would do. Maybe it was misleading, when I scooped her off the bed again (where she had sat again)—as if I were going to do a show and lift and move her all over the place.

"Hold it," she said at one point, sliding off from me. She came back with a camera. "I'm going to take a photo," she said. And she didn't simply snap the photo. She lined up the shot, down on her elbows, the camera tilting with interest, nosing toward me like a big black snout. I looked right back—sometimes I remembered all of my life in Tulsa, and I wanted to be alone, to go down onto the warm streets, to go to a bookstore. Anyway, I managed to hold it.

"We have to go buy condoms," she said, after the third time.

Of all the hundred errands we ran that summer maybe this was the primal one. In the end I made a big deal and told Adrienne I didn't want to go buying condoms at any of the drugstores my family frequented. It was a kind of made-up scruple—but I wanted to give her some idea of the embarrassment that was endemic to my heart. We drove west, across the river, and when the time came, we went through the line together. The cashier was an ashen-fleshed white woman. She didn't look twice.

"Now we're married," said Adrienne.

I overheard my mother using Adrienne's name on the phone.

"Adrienne Booker."

It caught me up. I stopped to listen.

"Booker. Mmhm. I think they are."

"I think so. I think he is."

"They're so young."

I had begun to live with Adrienne, almost. My parents didn't protest now when I spent the night out. I had wanted to call them, the first time I stayed overnight at the penthouse, but I fell asleep before I realized. Later I offered that my sleep-aways might worry them. My mom worked her jaw and said no, you need to be careful though.

But my behavior that summer had startled them, and they were being very watchful now, and were waiting. I knew this, and when I was out with Adrienne I often caught myself wishing that my parents could peer down like gods to glimpse this or that redeeming aspect of our lives. Adrienne's hyper-professional concentration in front of her easel, for one thing. Her rigor, the way she pinned me down in conversation and forced me to say what I meant. Our conversations over art books. The value of all this, and the adult seriousness. I even wished for them to know about things, all kinds of things, that did not make sense as parent-data: the way we knocked ourselves down dancing at a show; the world-weariness with which Adrienne held a cigarette when she was tired. Her tired voice, the grain of it. The balance of the long nights out, the sense of wayfaring endurance, as we journeyed from one destination to the next, and our delicate luck. Above all the profound sense of citizenship that, over and above personal pleasure, seemed to be the point of going to so many parties, every single weekend night.

Adrienne hadn't partied so much the summer before, she told me. The arc of her teenage life had already crested—painting was going to be a kind of second life: life after rock bands. But for me the life was only beginning.

I was nervous whenever we walked into a party. I thought she might veer completely away, to go talk to people I didn't know. I had to watch her to see what mode she was in. She drank either very little or else a great deal. In fact drinking provided an example of all I wished I could distill to turn into moral evidence for my parents. Formerly drinking had seemed to me like a sluice you could open and everything would flow. Adrienne was smarter than that. She marshaled her troops like a general. Often we were the most sober people in the room.

I looked up Adrienne's family at the library: I told

the librarian I was doing a research project on Booker Petroleum. I found out that Adrienne's great-grandfather, Odis Booker, first struck oil at a place called Cushing. This was in 1904, just three years prior to statehood. He eased out of wildcatting, built a large hospitality business, invested in local banks, and made a pile during the boom; he built refineries on the Arkansas and completed the Booker Tower in 1926. The penthouse was intended to impress and flatter clients from out of state. I even found a priceless newspaper clipping, from a 1926 edition of something called the *Chicago Herald-Examiner,* that included a photograph of our very bed, in black-and-white.

The building still housed Booker Petroleum. Today Adrienne's aunt Lydie, the same one who had gone to my college and whose garage Adrienne had burned down, worked downstairs, occupying the president's office. But we never saw her; we lived upstairs in a kind of elysium, or afterlife. In a cloud.

"Let's go down," I once said to Adrienne.

"What?"

"Just wander the halls," I said.

"Oh no," she said. Adrienne wanted nothing to do with Booker Petroleum. To the point that she revered it. It was a polished edifice, a memorial to the past. Gracefully acknowledged, and never to be desecrated—a reason to keep up appearances, at most. I don't think Adrienne really imagined her aunt did much, down there. There was no itch: Booker Petroleum tempted Adrienne neither as a lever of power, nor a source of resentment, nor even as a possible fate.

To a kid growing up in Tulsa in the 1980s, oil did seem very abstract. Every September, entering the fairgrounds, I passed between the legs of the Golden Driller, a statue who stood four stories tall, his concrete hand resting on a decommissioned oil derrick, his cartoonish boot the size of a small Japanese car. And I remembered that every Christmas my Galveston grandmother would sit me down so we could look at the Neiman Marcus Christmas catalog together. She had no sense of envy; she wanted to instill in me a sense of awe—I remember best the children's pages at the back of the book: an actual floating pirate ship for children, or preassembled Legos made into a life-sized knight and a dragon. But this was nothing compared to the stories my grandmother told about the boom times. Apparently in the sixties Neiman Marcus had his-and-her pontoon planes you could order, baby blue and pink, as if you were going to barrel into the sky like lovebirds the day you struck oil.

The oil refineries always occupied the opposite bank of the river. No one had ever explained to me how they worked—they were just a snake pit of detail that I pored over as a teenager standing with my bike on the pedestrian bridge, wondering what was important. I remembered an issue of *National Geographic* my dad kept, from the '78 oil crisis. Tulsa was on the cover, an aerial photograph of the refineries, lit up like a metropolis at night. In bright spots you could see the petroleum works illuminated, leaving dark reaches, I assumed the oil drums, in reserve. But I didn't know.

Adrienne showed me a videotape of her one parent—Rod Booker. "He lives in Rhode Island," she told me. In the video, Rod comes out a screen door, and stands in profile while it slaps behind him. He's a big bearded man wearing rolled-up khaki pants and an XXL black T-shirt. You can't tell what he's looking at: he seems to be looking away out of shyness, and when he finally turns and confronts the camera, it's like he's trying to stare it down almost. And it stays on him.

Then he turns again, and the camera pans and follows him down to the surf.

"That was my first movie."

Adrienne had wheedled a video camera out of her father when he left Tulsa. She was twelve years old and promised she would "use it to come visit him."

"Are you going there at all this summer?" I asked.

"I only went there that once."

I was a little shocked. Soon I requested the video again.

"Why do you want to keep watching the Rod video?"

"Boys have this thing about the girl's father."

She snorted.

Adrienne had never been anybody's daughter: Her biological mother, a Frenchwoman who spent American grad school on New England sailboats, abandoned the baby—Rod had had to book a flight to Tulsa and mix the formula, cradling the baby himself all the way, connecting in Dallas, changing her diaper on a toilet seat there, at last depositing his infant daughter at the ancestral home in Tulsa. After that, Rod felt his parental duties were fulfilled. He flew to Paris and spent some years trying to get Marianne back: their line to the family was that she had been suffering from severe postpartum depression. But young Adrienne would never see her mother again. Great-Uncle Harold, who at that time was running Booker Petroleum, was certain of that. He hired a string of Lebanese nannies, and his wife, Great-Aunt Alexandra, managed them.

Rod came back to live in Tulsa, but was often gone. Adrienne was closer to her great-aunt, a woman of Swedish extraction who had grown up in Nebraska and had met Harold at a ball in Denver. When she and Harold both died, Booker Petroleum passed to the younger generation. Rod sold his shares to his older sister, Lydie, and bought a house in Rhode Island in front of a rocky beach, not far from where he had first met Marianne. Rod had had so little to do with Adrienne that no one, when the time came, even suggested that she move to Rhode Island with him.

But Lydie must have been the least maternal woman in Tulsa. It was just the two of them, in the house on Twenty-eighth Place, not far from the Fitzpatricks': in only a year or two Adrienne grew quite tall, and started getting rides from older boys. She very wisely insisted on getting a motorcycle as soon as she was legal, which in Oklahoma is age fourteen. She started staying over at the uninhabited Booker penthouse: she would call Lydie in the middle of the night and say that she was drunk, that she should just walk over to the Booker rather than try to ride home. Lydie let it be known that Adrienne didn't have to call and wake her up every time she was drunk: she should just go to the penthouse as necessary. And so Adrienne moved there, bought new clothes, and decided she would never have to go back to Twenty-eighth Place again. She would drop school forms off in the inter-office mail if she needed her aunt's signature. She would order bagels and twenty-four-hour barbeque. She gave her laundry to the doorman, and her aunt paid. There was a janitor who came up to clean the bathrooms and take out the trash. Lydie was satisfied enough, and even set up a generous allowance for the sixteen-year-old, now that she was on her own. At least this is how Adrienne narrated it to me, when I kept her up one night, telling her about how much I cared for my own parents.

I accompanied her to the studio daily: Routine was an art. At the start of the workday she would change; she hung up her bright morningtime skirts very neatly, and once a week I would haul these back to the Booker for her and hand them off to the doorman like a stack of kites. I was proud of such chores. My writing went neglected. As the summer thickened and we started to sweat, I stopped altogether.

Adrienne and I circulated ourselves in the city. To be a painter, a mixed-media artist, and sometimes to be just a very wealthy young woman—to do all this you did a daily thinking up of needs, of paint and paintbrushes, new easels and even stools and chairs—of triple-pack men's undershirts and drop cloths and two-by-fours. In the beginning we would overlook the midday meal, but as the summer lengthened we learned to make an expedition out of lunch: we might get the lunch counter at Steve's Sundry to ourselves and order grilled cheese and egg salad, or we might admit that we were more in the mood for Village Inn, for raising our voices in that wide empty sea of plastic booths. Sometimes we set out for the eternally deserted eastside sushi place, where the rolls were enormous and loose. And then it was on to Hobby Lobby or Target or the lumberyard, or on odd days to the dealers west of the river, where we mingled with general contractors at specialty lock-and-doorknob shops or looked at fencing for no reason, or on one occasion purchased a hundred-pound chunk of limestone from a landscaper outlet. They refused to drop the rock into the trunk of my car but instead wedged it into the backseat because, they told me, "You wouldn't be able to lift it out of the trunk by yourself." The rock was deeply pocked all over, and yet smooth—like a human skull with eleven eye sockets. Adrienne helped me carry it up the brick stairs and into the corner of the studio, where it sat for the rest of that summer—and did her some good, I think.

We lived a beautiful life. Sometimes we drove around just to get ideas—Adrienne was painting squares then and she got her ideas from buildings. I asked, "Can you really look, with me beside you?" And she would cut me off: "Turn left, turn right." And then we would park. She was looking for lines, she said. She was trying to corner lines. The passing semis ironed out their shadows above an on-ramp under which the bike path dove, and anyone from my childhood could have driven by and glimpsed Adrienne, sitting on the hood of my car, sketching.

Cam went back to Connecticut in mid-July, more or less as planned, but it was a blow to Edith. I took her out to dinner, thinking I might now be in a position to introduce her to someone, to bring *her* into *my* world. Cam hadn't been very artistic anyway. "Adrienne and I stayed up all last night working on this minimalist sculpture she's making. It's a tabletop train landscape we bought, with foam hills and stuff, and we've covered it with nails. There's a nail exactly every square inch, you know?"

Edith didn't believe me.

"It's tedious," I admitted. "We get tetchy sometimes."

"You guys should just be having fun," said Edith.

But we were having fun. We went to the neon dealer one day. It was purchases like that that made me feel we were freer than two kids ever had been. Not just because we had Adrienne's money but because we had such a liberated sense of what to do with it. As a kid I had always looked out for the neon dealer. I was always driven past his triangular storefront, two glass walls, each canted to face to the street so that you had lit-up samples coming and going: Coke, Miller Lite, a neon toucan, a flashing domino. Seven or eight OPEN signs. But it never occurred to me that you would actually go into that store and buy something.

Sometimes that summer, when I looked down from the penthouse windows and saw midtown Tulsa in all of its tiny detail—the highways, the trees, the scrunched-up houses and neighborhoods—I was struck by how clear it was. I felt I understood how power worked. The complexity of a cityscape was supposed to intoxicate you, I knew, was supposed to exhilarate you with intimations of unseen connections and conspiracies. The city map was supposed to be like a powerfully overcomplicated circuit board: illegible, but richly suggestive, and downright functional, obviously. It was. It functioned very well. With Adrienne I felt I understood that.

Did it make me like Tulsa better, to date someone rich from it? Yes. It made me like it a lot better.

Yet from Adrienne I kept certain parts of myself back. Over and over she expressed interest in meeting my parents, I talked about them so much. But I wanted to keep her away from them. And there were certain parts of Tulsa. Like the Target store: the Target had been our standby when I was little. After dinner, on summer nights, my parents and I would go to Target. Just to stock up on things. But it was like a taste of ice cream, to drive and take a breath of that bright air-conditioned box. "Can I go ahead?" I would always ask as soon as we got through the front doors. I would run ahead to the electronics section, and my parents would pick me up there fifteen minutes later.

So whenever Adrienne needed Target for errands, I preferred to wait out front, pacing up and down the two hundred and twelve feet of sidewalk. I remember stopping once at sunset and watching for minutes as the sun went down, resolving into a visible red disk. I began to look directly at it—at the sun and then away. The setting sun was overwhelming the streetlight pole that stood between me and it, skinning the streetlight down into a little burnt stick. How hilarious, I thought, that I was trying to be a match for Adrienne Booker. She didn't know what this was, this florid fire. She was working in strict, massive shapes, in black-and-white gestures. My eyes were smarting: I loved the largeness of Tulsa, its big, summery fragrance, the asphalt, the puff of chemical air-conditioning that came when the Target doors slid open. And from the livestock barns, a lift of animal freshness.

Adrienne excused herself one night; a group of people had congregated at the Blumont, but she wanted to go home early. "I want to rest my voice," is what she said—meaning she wanted to be alone? I was going to stay and drink. I ordered a scotch I could barely afford and turned around in my barstool to survey the group. I wanted to know what it was like to hang out sans Adrienne.

Albert moved in on me almost immediately. In fact he sat down like I owed him something. He asked where I went to college. "So she's your adventure," he said. He nodded to himself. "You'll go back up there and tell the other guys about this crazy girl you hooked up with."

I wanted Albert to like me. It was intriguing to see a thickset fortysomething in his cups, rehearsing the kids' general grievances—that Tulsa sucked, that it had no confidence in itself, that it was an impossible place to produce real art. We often left him to the youngest kids (Jenny, in fact), and he was usually happy with that audience. I for one had never had a sit-down with him. I thought he must be curious, though: about me, Adrienne's new consort. He must wonder what sort of relationship we really had, how I did it, how I dated this undatable person.

But Albert was way ahead of me. "And then," he

continued, "after a while it won't be other men you tell about Adrienne, it will be women. At a certain point in every relationship, you'll roll out this thing about Tulsa and the 'one girl who almost made you stay.' Women will love you for it. It'll be part of your repertoire. Your 'Tulsa stories.'" He crooked his fingers to make scare quotes.

I got up to go, but Albert reached for me and held my arm in his fat fist. "You do know she's crazy, right?" I shook him off.

I arrived home that night not heeding the protocols I had recently devised, doing nothing to muffle my drunken homecoming. I started loudly drawing a glass of water in the kitchen, and then sprawled down in my adopted armchair in the front room. Earlier that day Adrienne had finally turned to me, while she was standing at her easel, and invited direct criticism of her work. I didn't hesitate for a second. I put my arm in, showing, almost touching her lines. I wasn't the nurturer Edith had been, encouraging me with my poems—nor was I merely playing at the language of criticism, as we did at school. I had been watching Adrienne closely, after all. And I thought she had been preparing me for this, a no-holds-barred criticism of physical response, intimacy, and confident trust. But she didn't thrill to the criticism. She didn't even really take it in. She seemed to have turned to me because she was genuinely worried about her paintings. She sat down after my crit and was quiet.

It may be that Adrienne's pictures were bad Franz Kline, that moreover her status at parties was a function of the naïveté of her milieu—Albert commonly referred to Adrienne as "the pope of the Brady District." And it may be that Adrienne's work ethic was only an exercise in girlish self-discipline. Sometimes I felt at once so robbed (as with Albert) and yet doubly possessed of my summer-long crush. I was sobered, in a way. Earlier that week my parents had announced that they might be retiring. They would retire together—Tulsa Public Schools was offering an early retirement package, trying to shed staff. My wise old parents were going to take it. And come next summer they would move to Galveston. That had always been the idea: to go be with my mother's people. And lately my grandmother had been very scattered and needed care, and my grandfather couldn't manage. It was time to circle the wagons. "And with you going away to college so far," my mother said. They might even move as early as March. And since we always had Christmas at Galveston, that meant that leaving for school in September might mean leaving Tulsa for good—I would never again have a parental excuse to come back here. I had to think about that. It was in this armchair where I was sitting that I had prepared Greuze and Chardin, and Delacroix, and Goya, for Adrienne. How long ago that seemed. It was as if all summer I had been staring out from the Booker hazily, and the stakes were only now coming into focus.

I had told Adrienne how I would stop some nights before I got home and turn the Camry's ashtray over into a neighbor's grass, running my finger under the tray's aluminum teeth to make sure all her ashes were gone. Sometimes if I had anything bigger—a wad of fast-food wrappers that we had failed to clean up, or beer cans—I knew a dumpster behind a McDonald's. I even threw my entire backpack away once, because it had been soaked in spilled rum. "Why don't you just tell them your girl-friend smokes?" she said. Which was, I think, the only time she ever referred to herself as my girlfriend. She repeated that she wanted to meet my parents. "They're your life," she said. "I should meet them."

We were at Target one Saturday. It was hot, the first Saturday of August. I had been waiting in the car. When Adrienne came back I told her I had an idea. My parents lived nearby and we could just go right now and visit them. She got back out of the car and went into Target. She came back with a new yellow sundress. She took off her T-shirt and shorts—feet on the dashboard, with people walking by—she put on the dress and reapplied her lipstick, and she was ready.

I had pulled out of their driveway only that morning. Now, my father was mowing the front lawn. "That's my dad," I announced. He was wearing a straw hat and jean shorts. When we pulled in, he did not stop, perhaps not hearing us, and we had to wait for him to get to the other end and wheel around before he saw us and let the mower die. He waved, and seemed to enjoy his predic-ament, stopping ten feet away to brush his hands off on his shorts. His beard would probably have been com-pletely white at that point. I remember being immoder-ately proud of him.

With Adrienne he was very charming.

I had never seen my father greet a strange young woman before. We were such a funny family. When I was little, it seemed that everyone we knew was old. And, as time went by, I had failed to bring in anyone new.

Of course as a teacher, my father would have met

new young men and women all the time. But this was different. He nodded just slightly as he shook her hand; he was already laughing. She said to him that he looked like me—so he got to do a double take and act a little surprised. I had forgotten that he could josh like this. Adrienne smiled, and insisted. She was careful to stand on the part of the grass that had already been mowed, as if to respect his work. She had a way with grown-ups.

He told her that I ought to be the one mowing the lawn, but that I was "too big" now to do so.

We went around back to put away the mower and my mom came out on the deck to meet us. I wished that Adrienne were more explosively beautiful. But my mom was very nice, of course, and sat us down on the patio furniture. I sat there rigidly, and I let the women talk. My mother's manner reminded me of when we used to run into her students—at the grocery store, for example, or once, when I was vulnerably twelve, into a whole gaggle of them at the fairgrounds. With teenagers my mother had an inimitable manner of noninsulting encouragement. She asked Adrienne about her upcoming gallery show—

"It's only a group show," Adrienne said. "But it's an honor to be included."

"You must be excited."

"Did you know that Adrienne's great-grandfather was a famous wildcatter?" I thought this might interest my mother, who sometimes taught Oklahoma history.

"Like from statehood days . . ." I prompted.

"I'd love to hear stories," she said to Adrienne.

"What ones I know . . ." Adrienne looked about, rueful.

My mother had thrown on something rather nice before she came out. And so how had Adrienne looked, from out the window? She looked so unconcealably pink, her pink throat and chin like a tall Russian teapot. Upright. I leaned back, to see if she had ripped the tag off her dress. She had. I was too young then to know how novel my parents were in the world. But I think Adrienne had divined their basic goodness already.

Galveston came up, and Adrienne poured out information about her childhood visits there. Booker Petroleum had big interests in Galveston. My mom and her tried to talk Galveston restaurants, though neither had heard of the others'. In fact my mother looked rather defiant, shading her eyes in the sun: she began to tell Adrienne, at length, about her brothers' and sisters' houses, and the neighborhood there, and the schools where some of my young cousins were enrolled.

I said that we had to get back, but my mother asked if I didn't want to show Adrienne through the house. It was a mess, she did say. I took Adrienne in through the back door, into the TV den, and I could hear Mom and Dad, through the thin outer wall, talking now about the yardwork. My mom was going to make stew for supper. Meanwhile, Adrienne had stepped up into the dining room, where family photos were ranged on a bureau. I felt a jagged upwelling of privacy when Adrienne stopped to look. "Come on," I said.

"Oh my god." She started to coo.

"Don't," I said.

Adrienne straightened up, burned. She waited for me to lead her around.

The house was not large, and soon there was no-where to go but into my bedroom, with Adrienne near my teenage bed—that was about the whole point, wasn't it? But she went straight to my green notebook, the one that I never took out of that room.

"What's this?"

"My diary."

She closed her mouth. Genuinely given pause, I think. She pivoted, and spent a few seconds admiring my bookcase. "I want to look at all your books," she said.

At the first intersection, with my car's AC still blowing hot air, I turned to Adrienne. Now we could relax—she had really been so perfect with my mother—surely she had some remarks to make, now that it was over—yet her poli-tesse was real. She had nothing but nice things to say about my parents. She really liked them. Especially my dad. But she turned on me: "You're being so strange."

"What?"

"You acted like you didn't want us to be there. I thought you were going to be so excited."

She was visibly upset.

"You acted like you were ashamed of me," she said.

Adrienne thought I was a great coward, sometimes. That made the difference between us. And everything else flowed from there.

There was the time she woke me up in the middle of the night and made me come out with her onto the Booker terrace. We were twenty stories high, recessed from the funneling wind. I heard a bat flapping in the gutter above us, a not-uncommon sound after dark.

103

"Watch this." She held out a pencil in her hand. The pencil was long and yellow and vertiginously shaved: she held it point-down, arm's-length over the rail. The wind was already nibbling it out of her fingers—between her pointer finger and her thumb, with her pinkie daintily up and clear—when she released it. "Uh—" The inclination to lurch over and watch, versus the horror of the clean skyscraper drop, screwed me off my sense of balance, and I imagined I had almost lunged after the pencil. I had seldom been pissed off so instantaneously. She continued to point down, her index finger right where the pencil had been. "That will be a new drawing," she said.

It was a fair conceptual point—

But I remember how it felt to lay my fingers on that railing and gingerly lean over and look. They teach you in science class that pennies dropped from on high can kill people. But no one was below, of course. Not in downtown Tulsa. The illuminated street, bobbing below me, was empty.

6

In August I got a piece of mail that for two nights lay unopened on my desk. On the third night I waited until my parents went to sleep and then closed my bedroom door and very silently unstuck the envelope. Inside was a pebbled piece of stationery stamped with the seal of the college registrar: "Request to Take a Leave of Absence."

Adrienne had started singing. The first time it happened I was laid out on the couch, reading; it was like she put down her paints and suddenly she was in front me, crooning—I was embarrassed. The song was a folk song. She met my eyes, but briefly. She did not want me to applaud. When she started a new song, I turned back to my book and pretended to read. She would practice like that, for fifteen or twenty minutes a day.

That August was hot. We would go driving, without purpose. I accelerated so gently and so seldom it felt like our front-wheel drive was a breathing animal, pulling us along in its animal thoughts. We were practicing our instincts. Often I didn't know—should I turn right, should I turn left? I was supposed to relax into the guesswork. One of the requirements of Sunday driving is that for long stretches no one speaks. It's a wholly kinetic form of pleasure. It was invented by farmers when they first got their cars. Maybe Adrienne had acquired a sense of it from art films, from their beautiful longueurs, and their discipline of boredom. The driver's seat is assumed by an uncle who doesn't talk much, one for whom silence is essential to the masculine condition. And maybe that was Adrienne's ideal.

One day we had come out to an area where we didn't usually get. We found an old fry house, and ordered chicken plates and malts. We ate in the car. Adrienne threw her bones out the window as she cleaned them. "Is that really what you do?" I asked. Adrienne nodded. She wouldn't speak—as if she was protecting her voice. It was getting more and more like that. I kept my bones on my plate, and then when I was finished walked all of our trash in, to the trash can inside.

Life was just a practice. I had come up the elevator that morning and crawled into her bed. We weren't feeling anything in particular.

"Here," I said, "I know this place." I pulled into a hardware store, its sunken parking lot vaguely familiar to me. "It's funny: all of these places, we're going to run into my dad somewhere."

But we ran into someone different. A buzz-cut guy in reflective sunglasses, explained to be a TU art student Adrienne knew. She shielded her eyes and engaged him politely. He had been gone all summer but was back now, getting ready for the semester. "Got to redo the studio space," he said. He grinned like a Cheshire cat and raised up the house paint he had bought—matte black, it looked like.

"Photography?"

"Portraits. I'm going to seat one good portrait a week, all semester long."

"Then you should do Jim sometime." Adrienne turned to introduce me. I don't know whether she realized what she was saying. Ever since July, when I had stopped writing, I had daydreamed about staying: becoming a regular, going back to Retro Night, for example—not dancing but somehow benevolently there, presiding. And around town, a man in my own clothes, gradually growing my father's beard. I could get a job of some kind. The Tulsan question: On those halcyon days you go out to lunch, what kind of car will you drive? Something respectable, I sensed. Or perhaps a pickup truck. A lanky, sad man. Jogging up and vigorously shaking someone's hand. At some kind of reception. At Adrienne's gallery show this fall, in my salt-and-pepper beard. Already faded with age. That could be two months from now.

One night I went home, and took off all my clothes, and filled out that form. I left it like a loaded gun in my desk. It would be the most prodigal thing I had ever done: to take a year off from college.

Meanwhile, Adrienne sang. I was no help; I knew nothing about music. I might take note, coming up from the street, of the voice as I heard it out the window, and of how it echoed in the stairwell. The timbre of it spoke to me more than the words. Her practice songs came from Alan Lomax recordings and old things, blues and staring, admonitory chants. I could hear the physicality of her courage in the open edges of her voice. She literally opened herself up and put her insides out there. I did not imagine someone of my temperament could do this. Adrienne was other. Sometimes, like someone teaching herself to cry on demand, she would scream. Just for a few seconds.

I came up behind her one day. I reached one arm over a shoulder, the other around her armpit, and held. I could feel it in her ribs how she worked, and in her skeleton how she strained to stand tall. She turned around in my arms and began a song where surely I would know the words. *O say can you see.*

I was supposed to sing along.

I did not want to do it. Adrienne always took me too literally. She never realized how hard I worked just *imagining* our relationship.

I did not sing along to the radio. Or in the shower. I had only intoned words lost in wide lumbering choruses at church and at school assemblies.

She held my eye. I breathed. She had gotten to "bombs bursting in air," the last word of which isn't really sung, but trembled out. Finally on "gave proof through the night" my voice found its center of gravity and bowled through the chute. Indeed my lungs were the best thing I had going, and as the song marched swiftly to its end, I realized I was using booming volume to cover for my lack of control. It was my lips and my tongue, my barely prehensile tongue, that I did not know how to use.

We did not say anything afterwards, but I felt better. We had not slept together in days, at that time.

Adrienne went to the small galley sink she had for her paints, and filled a glass of tap water. She drank half of it off, and when she finished she had to catch her breath.

"There's something I want to tell you about," I said.

And then it was too late, I had to tell her. "I have the chance to take a year off from school."

"What would you do?"

"Well. What am I doing now?"

Adrienne went over to switch her fan back on. "Is it to work on your writing?" she asked over the noise of the box fan.

"No, I mean—I *could* write. I—" Frustrated, I went over and turned the fan back off. I gestured. "It's obvious why I think of staying."

She sat down on the couch. "Jim. You know I've formed a band?"

"No. I did not know you had formed a band."

"That's what I was going to do when I started singing, Jim. I have a show this Saturday."

"I mean, this is fantastic. That's amazing."

She monitored my eyes. "You're upset though."

"I don't want to be."

"I'm doing something I can't share with you, Jim."

"Right."

"You need to think about what you can do."

That weekend I studied Adrienne onstage. I stood at the back and watched her performance with knowing eyes; I looked at her jeans, and watched for the wisp of irritation that sometimes crossed her face. She really did scream. She just stood up there and forced it, it was like she was exorcising something from her head. I knew how determined she was. There was a boy playing the harmonium, which I had just learned the name of, and a boy on drums. The music never overwhelmed itself—it wasn't supposed to be that she was upset, or that this was an access of passion. Her words didn't come from her heart so much as from other parts of her body, her diaphragm and her sinuses—and her perfect rib cage. This was the same corporeal apparatus that had been mine sometimes, that walked crabwise in bed, and roused me with its toe when it was hungry.

Maybe the thing Adrienne and I had really had in common was our selfishness. Within the scene, as I got it, the same audience went to every show, of every kind; some individuals thought there should be more shows, of any kind, period. The boosterism of the local arts pages, which never ran a negative review of any local band, even obtained in the bathrooms of the nightclubs, where if people talked to me while peeing I knew they wanted to be psyched, wanted me to be psyched. Most of all, they wanted Adrienne to be psyched. Those who remembered Adrienne's previous bands said so, and made themselves prominent enthusiasts of this, her return. She made none of them jealous, she was too much an alien for that. Her more pretentious fans talked about Adrienne's mystique. The younger kids kept their distance, but watched her like they might a passing legend, using itself up.

At bottom, perhaps, Adrienne was innocent of leadership. She had flair, and an artist's sense of what belonged to her. She never considered it a debit on herself to ask for something: negotiating with a club's owners to let her set an onstage table on fire, for example. (It was exciting, and then it took twenty minutes, her band stopped playing, and we all had to watch it; only Adrienne stood there, it was sublime and stupefying. It would not have worked in any larger town, but Tulsa was small enough to act like a furnace, reflecting its own light inward and reassuring itself, conserving heat.)

I had tried to love her by learning the way she lived. I liked it best when the summer blurred on me—whenever there was a good view of the skyline from someone's backyard, and I could raise my bottle in a toast. Occasionally I pulled off a good kiss, as difficult with her as a good joke. And the one time she let me up on stage with her I danced so wild I knocked an amplifier off, and the club made her stop, while they checked to see if it was damaged.

The first week of September was hot. Adrienne's studio had neither air conditioners nor many openable windows, and we only went there for an hour or so each day just to pretend we were working. At night her band came to practice. And day after day it stayed hot, summer didn't break, it kicked itself up another notch. Life melted. I started going back to the library sometimes, if only to enjoy its cool recycled air.

Adrienne wore a tiny charm from Chase, a shoe on a chain, which kicked against her chin when she was on all fours. For the first time, Adrienne let me mount her in her studio. We were not supposed to so much as caress each other during work time—even when we were very excited. But we gave up. She flattened a huge piece of cardboard and laid it down for us, and we slept afterwards with our bones on the floor. I remember waking up in the sun, in the fibrous reek of the cardboard, and finding myself alone, bargaining with God for just the sound of her voice behind me, or a clatter from the bathroom.

Adrienne had decided to record an album, working with Albert. They would do a session at Bartlesville in the fall. Painting had been an interval. She had stopped painting—the canvases were at Albert's gallery and would be shown in November, and she said almost nothing about them.

The scene thinned out. Life was slowing down. Or she might not work with Albert, she said. She might get a team of volunteers to help build a recording booth in her studio, once the weather cooled off. Chase could do it.

I spent more and more time in the wind. Up on the Booker terrace I liked how it was almost impossible to process or to think. Sometimes I contemplated putting a pin through a condom—while it was still in its wrapper so it would look safe. It was just a thought. The next skyscraper over and then down—my sight line swooped like a bird on the wing, imagining a glide, and a landing.

If I woke up first, if it was the type of morning that you might make breakfast in bed, I might instead (and she certainly didn't have any eggs) gather her laundry. I was riding down in the businessmen's elevator, dirty sleeves and panties forklifted against my chest. I had a real domestic emotion: Adrienne had performed the night before, she had been hoarse and very wonderful when she went to bed, teetering over her pillow and trying to ease down on her haunches, head hanging, like a pony who wants to spend the night in a human bed.

Sometimes the penthouse looked so trashed. These days were Adrienne's apotheosis. And I developed a repertoire of things I did, cushions I always straightened, lampshades I righted. I tried to keep the Turkish rugs flat. I became the one who always made the bed. Adrienne went to the studio without me, to sing, and I spent all afternoon in the penthouse. Or I went down to the streets and crept along the walls of the buildings. She had started using her motorcycle more, and sometimes from up in the penthouse I could actually hear it on the street below, in the deadly quiet of weekend evenings.

She was humorless, was why I liked her. Those last weeks she was spending more and more time with Chase, but I wasn't jealous, exactly. I did think she should see more of me. I thought she should paint more too.

You might suppose that I would force myself on top of her, that I would tell myself a story about reasserting our love. But when I tried my brute strength it only expressed how dumb I felt. And her cradling, crablike acceptance sometimes was equally, wonderfully dumb.

I went home to my father, once, and tried to spend an evening talking with him. I was just at that age, that summer, when you begin to appreciate that all the seemingly superficial things of the world have actual technical importance—that paint protects wood, as does dusting, that cleaning up after yourself is an essential instance of self-respect. And sometimes I would go to the penthouse and find its heirlooms slightly dirty. The Bookers had a Teddy-Roosevelt-style chair made entirely of nailed-together antlers, antlers grooved and seamed with gummy dust; I would sit down sometimes in it, measuring its creak as I lowered myself down. This was Rod's inherited chair, supposedly.

Once, when the apartment was getting very cluttered, I went out and put six bottles of Adrienne's favorite whiskey on her credit card. One of the six bottles went in the double-doored wardrobe, thrust into the leg of a boot. One I planted beside the tub, among shampoo bottles. One in a trash can in the study. One in plain sight on the hearth. One on the terrace, which had a built-in liquor cabinet we never used. And one in the refrigerator door.

I started to stay up all night at the penthouse. Adrienne would turn over in her bed. I would prowl around, fixing things, straightening. Whoever designed it really was fantastic, the big fireplace up this high like for a hunting lodge in the sky. I could put a pillow on the hearth and lean back, and obliquely out the terrace windows catch the eastern sky lightening.

One night I thought I heard the elevator ding. It was nothing, but I froze where I sat. I thought Rod Booker would come in, or his dead grandfather Odis, either one of them to kick me out, or to make me finally introduce myself.

Adrienne had talked about coming to the airport with me. But I was not sure I had given her the date of my

114

departure. And when it approached, I didn't call her. I had not called her for several days. My heart was tired. I thought I might try to disappear, and not force her to write a speech and kill an ox.

My parents were circling tighter. There was much for them to do, buying me a new laptop, stocking me up on allergy medicine, buying socks. I was reminded how much I needed them. They had to cosign my student loans. Shopping for the laptop with my father, I was struck by how fun life could be. My father and I had a certain amount of money to spend, we weighed the different bundles and options. I told him about some of the different classes I was considering taking. It all made sense to him.

But right before we sat down to dinner that night, the phone rang. "Weren't you going to call me?" Adrienne asked.

"So, Adrienne's going to take me to the airport tomorrow," I told my parents. They understood—skeptical as they were of Adrienne, they imagined the love we had was as big and round and pink as any teenagers'. They would give any scene at the airport a wide berth.

I budgeted thirty minutes to say goodbye. Picking up Adrienne at two, I would have us to the airport with time to kill. She would take a taxi back, and my parents would get my car out of short-term parking that same day. The inconvenience for my parents mortified me.

In the event, Adrienne was late coming down. The Booker's shadow was chilly, and I got goose bumps waiting in the car.

She dressed casually that day. Her T-shirt, tucked

into her beltless jeans, puffed out, so that it was like a small cloud floated in and occupied my passenger seat.

"We're late," is all I said.

When the tongue of the highway lapped us up and locked us in and drew us on the highways that ran like aqueducts out of the ancient city of Tulsa, I gathered myself up and thought: This could be the last time. Downtown, and then the green neighborhood of my elementary school, had already fallen away behind us, and the cityscape to come was a haze. Homes, billboards, fast food, furniture emporia, I had not memorized it any better this summer than I ever had before. Tulsa would always be indifferent. The only thing that distinguished me today was in my passenger seat: Adrienne Booker, the famous girl. After my parents moved I would have no excuse to come back here unless Adrienne bade me, and she wasn't going to do that.

Adrienne wanted to help me with taking my luggage out of my trunk, but I yanked it all out myself and started walking. She hurried to keep up; she tried to catch my eye. But this was how I wanted her to remember me. I decided to check every single piece of my luggage. That way I walked beside Adrienne empty-handed—better, I thought, to go with no reading material into the future.

"Jim," she said. We were stopped beside the newspaper dispensers, in sight of my departure gate. "I can go sit with you. Or I can turn around here. I don't know how you like to say goodbye."

I had to reel and take stock of the people around me. They were not my friends. Not that I disliked, for example, the man passing by in the ocher plaid shirt, but he had made a deal with his homeliness that I would never be offered—no more than he would ever appreciate why I had invested so much in my own vanity, or how deeply in the red I now was. How dare Adrienne ask me what I wanted? I wanted her to be here, and to act on her own needs. She acted like she was here only politely, to service me. "I am going back to college," is what I said.

She was puzzled. Did she not realize what a fool I had felt like, all summer long?

I pecked her on the nose. "Good luck with your recording," I croaked.

So I sat at my gate alone. This was my last look at Tulsa, and I could not even see it: out the window it was only tarmac and sky, like the whole city had slid off the table. I prayed for the power of memory to preserve it. More important than saying goodbye to Adrienne, I told myself, saying goodbye to the town. Because of course what I told myself was that I was graduating—that, one year out from high school, this was the real commencement.

PART II

1

I went back to college and I made a lot of friends. I was older now—I wore my newfound bohemianism like an old coat, partaking of joints with a companionable ease. Clinking my glass. I hardly forgot Adrienne. For a while I sent her emails, but I never got a correspondence going. Either Adrienne didn't reply or she typed off something careless. "You are the philosfer," was the sum total of one of her answers, after one of my best, most excited emails. It was like she bent over her keyboard without even sitting down, typed something, and was off. Whereas I sat up all night building my paragraphs. When I pressed send I slipped out of the dorm and went brooding over the email I had just written, down sidewalks and river trails. And when it rose, the morning sun smelled like acorns and dirty jeans. I went home and slept. I was not unhappy. In fact, the last emails I sent were written in full knowledge that Adrienne wasn't even reading them. Like skywriting: the words fade, and the little biplane stutters off over the horizon. I stopped emailing at the first freeze. Stopping seemed to me an essential gesture. And then after that I tried not to think about her too much. Not because it hurt. But because I needed to hide from Adrienne, in my mind.

What would she say, if she ever ran into me again? After I graduated, and moved to New York, I became obsessed with this possibility. That maybe Adrienne would see a sobered man, with his face set against her. Or someone who three years on still had something to say to her. I had moved to New York, as most kids do, with a dire sense of fate and culmination, and I was prepared to meet Adrienne around any street corner. I would spy her down the block, at the point just before a face gets legible. Not that I really planned to see her. But she ghosted the ins and outs of all my yearning: my poems, my job, even other girls. Sometimes I hardly registered her among my thoughts, but she was there—even in college I had used Adrienne, like a kind of high C, to put my head into tune.

In New York I got paid exactly $207 a week to work at a big literary magazine—part-time, to be sure, though it took up most of my days. Some people said it was criminal for them to be paying me so little, with no benefits. But the name recognition was big. As everybody acknowledged. And I was happy to work with so many famous writers—meaning I typed them correspondence about their payments. I got up early every morning and put on nice pants and tucked in my shirt. I thought of Adrienne: her early mornings, with her skirts. I wished she could see me when I climbed up from the subway at Times Square. Now here was a wide-awake city. Here was a downtown.

I wasn't writing. I partied a lot. Literary New York was a round of parties. But you couldn't quite feel that they were leading anywhere, the way parties in college did. Or in Tulsa. In Tulsa we drove all night across town to get to a party, feeling as if it was going to be of historical significance when we got there. That was what made weekends fun. We had kidded ourselves— but properly. Now I was merely a dupe. Living on $828 a month.

I had discovered, on my computer at work, that if you center an online map on North America and dial down to the local level, zooming in without reference to region or state, it's Coffeyville, Kansas, that loads. I had been to Coffeyville. I hadn't known though that it was our nation's bull's-eye, the center of America. On-screen it's basically an intersection of highway above a pale green fill—but then at the bottom of the screen I saw that there was a tempting white border, and that clicking south on the compass I could cross down into Oklahoma. I clicked and let the screen redraw, following the most eye-catching line, bright yellow Route 169—down through blankets of farmland, through the pale emptiness around Nowata, and down further till, trending westward, past Talala, past Oolagah, 169 made a confident westward leap over Owasso, and the computer seemed to have to stop and think, to gather itself, before Tulsa displayed.

Meanwhile, my parents' lives went on like ancient chronicles. In Galveston a young uncle flew his pickup off the road, and I went to Texas to be in the waiting room when he died. My grandmother died too. My twenties were stitched to life by these funerals. And I

123

would forgo a party in New York for a funeral in Texas any day of the week. Texas and that part of the country, Oklahoma, that was where reality obtained. Two different cousins got divorces. One of them turned out to be badly in debt, and before we knew anything my grandfather gave her $40,000 out of his life savings. Shortly after that we got power of attorney over him, and put him in a home.

I missed Tulsa, but was getting used to Christmas in Texas, the Christmas lights strung above the sand—I tried calling a girl I was seeing to tell her about it. I walked away from the family bonfire with my phone on my ear. A little boy came skittering out of the blackness. He was my second cousin. I was talking to my "girlfriend." I was trying to tell her how good it was to get away from New York, into the largeness of the night.

I didn't stick with any girl—I wasn't writing. I seldom got up sufficient momentum to feel that it was even me, Jim Praley, who kept coming back to his desk. Sometimes on a slow night I tried to tell someone about Adrienne: I knew it was a good story. But I never emailed Adrienne, or tried to make contact. For long periods of time I probably didn't even think about her: we all have these recurrent dreams in our lives, which we manage mostly to repress. There was once, early on, when Edith came through town and I took her out to some bars. I made a point of not even mentioning Adrienne's name, not once. "That girl Edith was worried about you," my roommate later reported.

"Why?"

"She said you used to be a lot nicer."

I was trying to get a full-time job somewhere, I was trying to figure out what to do in my life. Still, sometimes, coming home of a winter's afternoon, when my mind ought to have been full of all kinds of things, and I was trudging through the snow, I looked up to see if Adrienne might be waiting there on my stoop. As if Adrienne of all people would struggle up through five years of absence to come and sit in the snow.

Once, on the train home, I thought I saw her, a very prim girl seated in the next section. I flattened my back to the door, my heart pounding, and as the train reentered the tunnel I fought to catch her reflection in a window. She got out at the first stop in Brooklyn, and I raced out too, I ran up the steps and followed her above ground, keeping a certain distance between us—her blond hair done in a complicated chignon and her step, amazing, brisker than ever—until I saw that I was going to lose her and began to trot, and actually sort of let her get away, crossing to the opposite side of the street as she, whoever she was, disappeared behind a sliding glass door.

When I got news of Adrienne's accident I had just turned twenty-four. It was a cool day in September; I was getting ready for work, but I had stopped what I was doing to yank out my window unit. It was just the one window, in that room, and I had not been able to open it all summer.

Even though I was running late now, I stood by the newly opened window enjoying it. I decided to read my email. Something had come in during the middle of the night, and there were already four or five responses on top of it. It was the high school listserv, of all things. Somebody had been hurt—I scrolled down.

Many of you will remember Adrienne Booker, who went to Franklin with us through the eleventh grade. Adrienne was involved in a serious car accident yesterday morning. She is going to be okay, but has temporarily lost the use of her legs. She was riding her motorcycle. Her spine was broken in two places. The spinal cord itself was bruised. But the doctors tell us that Adrienne was lucky, if the spinal cord had been cut, we would not be able to hope for recovery at all.

Adrienne has been a vital member of the Tulsa community for many years. I know some of you have already visited her. I can't be there today, but I wanted to do what I could to help spread the word. Adrienne's family tells me they can be found in the intensive care unit at St. Ursula's in Tulsa.

Please forward this message to everyone. Visitors are welcome.

Chase Fitzpatrick

I read that email before I knew what it was. Launched into confusion, I feared that I had written the email myself, somehow. I reread it quickly twice just to make sure she wasn't dead. I tried to get clear what had happened. I didn't understand. That her life had been going on all this time, but now she'd fucked up. And therefore we all found out about it, online.

I wasn't even crying. I swayed there, with my elbows on my desk. A broken back was not good. I rubbed my eyes. And then I sat down. In fact, I started reading the *New York Times*. For years I'd had the restraint never to google Adrienne. There had been a line. I did not search for her.

I read an article about Congress, clicking even to the second page. And then I stood. I leaned my forehead on the raised window sash. I was going to miss my train. I would force myself to picture her injury. The bones very visibly snap, and the nerves go dark. Fine. It was a cartoon, a diagram. I visualized her real arm. It was sticking out in mental space, the fist hard and the wrist straining, the little arm hairs translucently raised, and the muscles of the forearm compact like a fish. As if only her arm had been broken in the crash.

I realized I was crying. For years I had been visualizing her face only. But finally I had figured out what belonged to me: I struck my forehead hard against the glass. Sometimes you want the world handed back to you. And on the penthouse terrace, reaching her arm away out with that pencil between her fingers. As if she had taught herself to throw the world away.

I didn't go in to work that day. This was going to be Adrienne's gift to me. I called in, and told my boss what I was going to do: that there was an open flight leaving in ninety minutes, and that if I made it I could be in Tulsa by lunchtime.

In the taxi on the way to JFK, with my common sense in tatters, I was blinking, passive, calm. I fingered the buttons on my cell phone. I was gone—I sat stunned, watching the New York streets run by. I couldn't hear the radio. And I hadn't been to Tulsa in five years.

With delays at the airport, I might have taken time to sit and rethink, but I docked my laptop and plunged into email again. The list had blown up: old classmates felt obligated to quickly type something, to demonstrate their dismay, to wish Adrienne well. Now that I had time to study the thread, I discerned that my onetime friend Jamie Livingstone had, less sensationally, entered another hospital that same day—he for an obscure bone treatment. Together with Adrienne's wreck this set everyone going. People undertook chronologies of all respectable alumni suffering, of early deaths, of parents' deaths, of injuries, of house fires, of layoffs, piling onto each other's lists in what was condoned as a grief ritual. But really it was a kind of victory lap—we had lived, and we could prove it. The real world had made its visitations. It hadn't complicated us—on the contrary. All the codes of speech, the terror of the popularity system, the guarded egos, all that stuff had slipped away. We were very nice to one another now.

I was still reading after I boarded the plane. The stewardess asked us to shut our laptops and slide down our window shades—so that thereafter the shades glowed, heavy with the morning sun. I sat with my head bent, already tired, waiting. Once we reached cruising altitude, I pulled my laptop out again. There had been a total of fifty-three downloaded messages since early this morning. And yet none of them came from anyone I remembered as

Adrienne's friend. Nowhere on the listserv did anyone address my questions: What had been the cause of the wreck? What did the doctor say her life would be like, if she really couldn't walk? And what exactly was meant by "Adrienne's family"? "I can't believe this is all happening," one Kim Wheel had written. Kim Wheel, the girl who did the morning announcements senior year. What did Kim Wheel know of Adrienne? "Was at St. U's last night. It is so amazing how people come together at times like these. We're so glad that you are going to be all right, Adrienne, and we are all going to send you our energy." As if Adrienne was ever going to check this list.

I shut the laptop. Pinned upright in the seatback pouch was a Brooks Brothers sack—that sheep, hoisted in the air. In the departure lounge with ten minutes before boarding I had got up and bought Adrienne a green Brooks Brothers necktie, thinking it would be fun to bring her a present. I now very carefully withdrew the sack and slid the necktie out and, bowing, eased it around my neck. I move in slow motion when airborne. The air is so thin. I always ask: If this plane crashes, what will I have to show for myself? If Adrienne crashed, I could crash too. Today's flight was the most random and at once possibly the most fated plane ticket I had ever purchased. And if I died no one would have a clue, I would be inexplicable. I was making a gesture towards Tulsa, a fling. My parents would never figure out what exactly I had been up to—the arc of their wondering, however, suited me. This last-minute airline ticket had cost me $647, which was most of my checking account—the necktie had cost $59. The taxi $35. With all this I blew

October rent and disbalanced my finances for the fore-seeable future.

At Tulsa, my green bag was not on the carousel. I had packed lightly, but only owned the one oversized duffel. I had just been glad that morning that Marcus had still been asleep when I rolled it out into the common area. He was a good roommate, but I hadn't been in the mood to discuss it all with him. I should call him though, later.

The sun was jammed between the glass walls of Tulsa International, and it smelled like dust. I waited. I let the carousel click each time and push itself around. My fellow passengers all took their luggage and left.

Almost socially I went into the baggage office. The clerk was younger than me and didn't get that I wanted to make friends with him; he glumly went into the back and returned dragging the bag itself. "It came in earlier this morning. Where are you flying out of?"

"New York—but it was on a last-minute deal, I flew United to Dallas, and then American here."

"That's why. They routed it through on a different connection."

I had half wanted to lose the bag—I didn't look forward to entering the hospital dragging it behind. But here it was. It was mine.

I had starved myself at DFW, so I had some cash. I could move however the ground transportation pre-sented itself—I had the romantic notion that I could take the bus. As if I thought there was public transportation in the postwar American city. But at the car rental place

I made a sentimental request: "Do you have anything like a Camry?"

The dashboard was updated, pudgy. The Camry of my teenage years had been lean. I could barely afford this rental and would have to return it early the day I left, two days from now. Meanwhile there would be lots of free food at the hospital. I buckled up, I enjoyed my seat; Tulsa's traffic map came together in my head. I rolled down my windows once I got out of the garage and I breathed in the fresh, unremembered air—had I been a better person, when I lived here? It was just out past this access road that Adrienne and I had gone to that gay bar. Now I got up heading south on 169 in the early-afternoon glare, keeping the downtown skyscrapers to my right, and accelerating. From the plane I had spotted the Booker—the car shuddered with my window down, the air buffeted across my mouth. My high school was already miles behind me when I became aware of the neighborhoods of my middle school crushes ahead: A spray of feeling around Forty-first street. And then Fifty-first street. The whole time it was almost like someone was watching me—I had to jerk hard right, scudding across a median to make the St. Ursula's exit lane.

I had not had time to think. The flight had been too short. Only seven hours ago I had stopped to check my email, oblivious of fate. I slowed down, and tried to prepare. I had been going over it on the flight from Dallas: "I heard what happened, and I wanted to come." But there would be other people there, wouldn't there? I had to act casual: "I got this for you at Kennedy. I was getting ready for work when I got the email." Always I had imagined Adrienne would seek me out, or fate would deliver her to me at random. I hoped she would just understand. Maybe it would go like this: she would see me and smirk, and I would smirk, and then I would approach the bed with the necktie sack: "I brought you a tie, Adrienne."

St. Ursula's Hospital was built on a rise, a modern pink V-shape, bending at a shallow angle, looming up against the highway like one section taken out of a pale pink Pentagon. Bradford pears were planted around. Against the pink wall the leaves looked black.

Once I parked I suddenly relaxed. Here I was. I knew my way around. In line at the water slide out south I had used to gaze up at St. Ursula's—the distant landmark, the futuristic castle striped with windows. I locked my doors. Once I entered the hospital I knew I'd lose Adrienne in a certain way, as a mental prop—I ought to take a deep breath. At the desk, I had to pronounce her name. It was hard to do. An ex-girlfriend, by definition, is a memory improperly possessed. But it was out of my hands now.

The elevator down suspended me, and then the floor dinged. I was grateful to know that Chase wouldn't be there. Maybe Edith? Maybe Adrienne's aunt Lydie? Whatever happened, I was armored, sombered—the doors rumbled apart and revealed a vast waiting room, filled with families. You could tell they were families. I proceeded in, dragging my huge green bag behind me, angling into the recesses of the waiting room, nine or ten couchlengths deep. People before me had come bearing gifts: I saw care packages, baskets of fruit, and paper bags thoughtfully stashed with blankets and Gatorade and crossword puzzles. Most people were on the phone, giving a report to someone somewhere else. They were mothers and aunts and sisters: they all had full rights to the stories they were telling.

A man I definitely recognized as Rod Booker was there. He was off to the side. But I rolled on, pretending not to know him. I barreled around the perimeter of the waiting room, dragging my bag on its side to slip between various encampments, lifting my necktie sack clear. Eventually I came up behind him and dropped my bag. When he didn't turn, I poked his shoulder. It was like poking a ham.

So this is your father: he stood; he reached his elbow back and reared himself up. He was slow in his bulk, but finally turned out to be taller than me. A furry-faced buffalo with wide blue eyes and a nose like Adrienne's. There were moles and other kinds of spots falling down into his snow-white beard.

He wouldn't make eye contact.

"Mr. Booker? Jim Praley."

"You're here to see Adrienne?"

I nodded.

"Well, come on." His passage through the couches was slow and deferential. He let a kid making realistic spluttering sounds drive a Hot Wheel on the carpet ahead of us. I was carrying the necktie sack under my armpit.

"Have a lot of people been around?" I asked.

"There were a lot of you last night," he said. Exiting the waiting room we seemed to enter a maze of lonely laboratories, but Rod knew the way. He stopped and depressed a wall-mounted plunger, and down the hall two oversized doors unlocked and began to swing apart. I kept telling myself how I would look right at Adrienne and not look away no matter how disfigured she was: that she was badly hurt, and that holding her eye and carrying on a conversation might be a real achievement.

And what would Rod think when he witnessed this reunion? After all, I probably knew his daughter better than he did. This must be the most time he had spent with Adrienne in a decade. But he went on ahead of me, like a humble bear.

He led me into a small bay commanded by a nurses' desk and cluttered with empty gurneys and beds. Five or six units opened off of it; all were occupied except the one that Rod stopped in front of. It was lit up extra-bright, like a nightclub after close, with a worker inside, mopping.

Rod hollered out, "Did you move her already?"

The janitor looked up, frightened—he didn't understand English.

I veered off into the flotsam of loose beds, as if I knew something Rod didn't. And here she was.

2

They had her out in the hall, on a tallish gurney about level with my diaphragm.

Her eyes were masked, her neck was braced, and the rest was sheeted.

A seam of white spittle, like fat on a refrigerated roast, lay between her lips. Under the edge of the eye mask, her skin had swollen up the color of graphite and then was drawn, in awful melting rills, to her ear. She was unconscious, but her lips were grim and full of knowledge.

It was by her nose that I recognized her.

Rod went to the head of the gurney and tried his hands on its corners. He puffed up his cheeks and gazed down at Adrienne, and then sighed ever so gently, blowing on her cramped hair.

"Is she awake?"

"She won't be awake for days, my friend."

I was shocked. It maybe made sense that Adrienne be blindfolded, as if she couldn't face her fate. But the rest of it—the snarl of bedsheets, with intravenous bladders resting between her legs—I could not believe that it was so real. I could not believe that Adrienne was fundamentally, internally hurt.

Rod had walked around opposite me, and spread his arms out along the length of her bedrails. "She's a fighter," he said.

"Yes," I said.

"Where are you coming from?"

"New York. Are you still in Rhode Island?"

He glanced up, surprised. And then he nodded.

"She used to show me a video. She made it when she was like twelve."

He thought for a second, and then nodded. "That's right. She visited me—"

"It looked like a beautiful location—"

"But you came all the way from New York?"

"Yes."

"That's amazing." He shook his head, and seemed to return to his study of Adrienne's condition. "That's really a tribute." He began trying to manipulate the gurney. Its wheels were locked. He was idly fumbling at them with his big blunt boot when a male nurse appeared, carrying a roll of blue tape.

"Sorry, Kevin and I are going to do this." He stepped into Rod's space, and started taping down the wires that led out from Adrienne's monitors, also bundling together the IVs and something else—a catheter or something.

"Let me help," Rod offered.

The nurse ignored him.

I was thinking about the time Adrienne and I went

shopping for a block of marble. There was a home-and-garden place that had some. But Adrienne insisted on hefting each piece in her own hands, and the clerk almost wouldn't let her. He kept easing each piece back out of her hands. Adrienne finally told the man, "You have to just go away for ten minutes, and when you come back I'll buy something."

Rod had come over to my side. With the nurses right there, he put his lips up to my ear and whispered, "My sister doesn't think she should be moved."

"Is it tricky?"

"Well, she shouldn't be bumped. My sister thinks they need this bed, is why they're moving her."

"And—your sister, that is Lydie?"

"Mmhm." Rod was approaching the gurney again.

"Watch the mask," said the nurse, "the mask is important. Would you hold this?" the nurse asked me.

"Yes," I said, not expecting the bag of milky fluid he was already handing me. When I lifted it to clear its tube from the others, I discovered the tug of resistance that came, I hated to think, from some part of Adrienne's skin. So I held it resolutely, overhand, arm unwavering.

There were now four men matching pace as we launched into the corridor, Adrienne floating between. The mask pressed around her eyes, its padding like a lovingly folded washcloth. I loved her. The radiating wires and IV sacks floated after her like a train, and only Rod had nothing to carry. I wondered if I should feel sorry for him.

Crowding everyone else to the walls, we pushed Adrienne into the elevator, where her gurney stood like a raised banquet table. But everyone looked away. Only one woman, an African-American woman with a diplomatic bearing, looked at Adrienne with steady sympathy—and forcefully, as if Adrienne needed people to look at her. I myself looked at the parts of Adrienne that weren't hurt, her good skin, the normalness along her nose, the total normalness of her now-uncovered arm. I really didn't know where to look. I tried to smile at the woman who was being so nice; I looked up and away, at the counting numbers above the door. But it was taking a while, I had to relent, and swung my eyes back along Adrienne's bed. Her one arm was in the cast, but the arm near me had come uncovered somehow and was bare, palm-up, soft, clammy, the fingers curled. I asked myself if I ought to take Adrienne's hand, if that might be the thing I had come all this way to do: to take just that liberty. I would fly away before she ever woke up or was cognizant—I would just squeeze her hand, and go. But then the elevator dipped on its cable. The doors started to shake, and were pulled aside with an almost insidious swiftness.

Lydie stood there. Her hands were linked in front of her, hanging, and she smiled impatiently as we paraded to Adrienne's new room. The nurses relieved me of my milky bag and brushed us away; the transfer was swift. From the doorway I watched as four or five nurses managed to scroll Adrienne sideways, without bumps. I noticed that one of them reached for a cord dangling from Adrienne's leg and immediately plugged it in. A loud ticking sound ratcheted up, and was relieved by a whoosh. Lydie stepped forward, also curious, and lifted the sheet—Adrienne had been fitted with white plastic leggings, each divided into pouched sections, each pouch alternately deflating and then inflating, moving up and down the patient's legs like a slow, plastic massage. "To prevent blood clots," the nurse said.

Once Adrienne had been straightened in her bed and the nurses left, Lydie turned on Rod: "So here we are."

He took off his hat and scratched the back of his head; he gave me a look.

Lydie was an impressive woman. Tall enough to support a mane of silvery black hair that didn't quite overrun the bounds of seriousness, her stance was mannish, with one foot pointed out and her fist on her waist like a Shakespearean player. Her ankle-length shift was unbelted. The way she looked at Rod, balefully, seemed very much in character with her features: a blunted nostrilly nose, and wrinkles indicative not of tiredness but of warm endurance, running down in swoops from her eyes and nose. Her lipstick was frankly and neatly applied, and she wore eyeliner that, in an owlish way, worked. "We're never going to get transferred back down, you know. The only way back into ICU is in an ambulance."

Rod lowered himself into a chair. "That's what you do—if the doctors screw up, you call and get a new ambulance and you start over."

Lydie shouldered her purse and made ready to leave.

"I'm pretty sure they know what they're doing here," said Rod.

"But what they are doing is running a business, Rod. I have total confidence that they know what they are doing. They're shuffling beds." She turned to me. "Were you going to come with me to get hamburgers?"

Lydie and I left the hospital via skybridge. I had not yet reintroduced myself, yet she seemed to have me well in hand. She was a regal walker with long strides, and her shift beat against the backs of her ankles. At the end of the skybridge she raised her hands against the door in front of us, relying on her momentum to open it:

And everything changed. The hospital's bright air-conditioned interior shrank to nothing. It was like walking out of a movie: The garage darkness was damp and fresh. The gasoline opened my nostrils. You could hear the muttering of one or two cars moving on the floor below; there was a drip someplace, far away, all around us.

Lydie stopped, and glanced keenly into the darkness. Then she raised her key chain and fired, and in the darkness a car winced and blinked its lights.

We strode forward.

"I hope I'm not stepping on your toes," I said.

"What do you mean?"

"Being here today."

"I fight with Rod because if you don't, he'll drag everything into the ditch. You have to fight him."

Out of politeness, I pretended to be confused: "He's the patient's father?"

"He fathered her."

With my hand on the door handle I waited for her to get in, but she was fishing for something in her purse. "Well," I said, "I really hope she recovers."

"Uh-huh. Listen—"

I had to get in the car to keep up with the conversation. The car reeked of cold leather.

"She's going to recover." Lydie depressed the cigarette lighter. "She doesn't have any other choice. We do have to be careful though. I don't think neuroscience is the strongest branch of medicine. Do you? And St. Ursula's isn't the Mayo Clinic. I can't believe they had you carrying that IV pouch. I'll be able to sue them for that alone. And her father goes along with everything they say . . ."

"He has a doctor's-orders mentality."

"Uh-huh. But sometimes you have to press." Lydie held up both hands, heavily bejeweled, and shoved gingerly into the air between us.

"The path of least resistance," I added.

Lydie smirked, and the cigarette lighter popped. She produced a pack of cigarettes.

"No thanks," I said.

"Mrmm." She held the unlit cigarette in her lips and brought the red-hot coil up, and sucked at it with the cigarette like a straw. She puffed. "Adrienne's worst injury is so low that, even if she didn't recover, she'd be able to walk. She's S2. Are you familiar with this terminology?"

"I'm not."

"Well, *S* means sacral." Lydie backed out and then paused, with her long car crooked in the lane. "Anyway, the sacrum. That's the term for the end of the spine, the triangular piece of bone there." She measured it with her fingers, and then snapped them. "That's shattered. And the cord there is bruised." She leveled her eyes at me. "It's the part that controls the bowels." Lydie shrugged and stared, seemingly distracted, into the windshield. "Above that, however: T7. The seventh thoracic vertebra. Controls the legs. The bone there didn't shatter, but was snapped in two, and one of the pieces is slicing down and pinching the spinal cord. We want to slide that piece back up before it slips further, and staple it to the other piece—to keep it from doing any further damage. We want to take the pressure off that section of the spinal cord. In time, it should come back to life, and she'll be able to walk. Anyway, they're going to do surgery tomorrow, to stabilize the bone there, as well as parts of the neck where she has hairline fractures. It's just a preliminary surgery— to stabilize her. But until then they should be keeping her in ICU. She needs to be constantly monitored."

Was I supposed to have spoken up when they came to take Adrienne away? I wondered if Rod had secretly wanted me to. Somehow in coming here I had assumed that Adrienne was ultimately okay, that paralysis was just a matter of being knocked out and then waking up. "How did it happen?"

"In the first place Adrienne should have gone to St. Luke's—that's where we would normally go. But of course I got the call in the middle of the night, that they had her here on life support. I called Rod. 'Your daughter has been hospitalized,' I told him. And he did come. However he's still the most *passive* person I have ever dealt with."

"Right."

"We have to decide on surgeons here. Then we have to decide on rehab programs. And that means researching different therapies."

"Huh. Is there anything exciting there?"

"But Rod takes no interest. You do. You take more

interest than Rod does, and he's her legal guardian. I'm the one"—Lydie pressed her fingertips into her sternum—"who is going to take care of Adrienne if she doesn't get up. While my brother, as I'm sure he told you, is *devastated*."

"Well it's pretty traumatic."

"It's a nightmare." She raised her eyebrows intimately. "It's an absolute nightmare."

Lydie had straightened us out and reversed, executing an eccentric but practiced maneuver, backing the car quite elegantly past the ramp, backing against the arrows until she was lined up with the exit and could sail right out. It was efficient, high-handed, and fluid. I thought Lydie used to have a driver. But she drove for pleasure, apparently.

Lydie followed the hospital's landscaped drive, snaking up to Sixty-first Street, and we sat there with her blinker on, clicking for a turn. New York loomed in my imagination, the work I was missing, a drinks date I had tonight at one of my favorite bars—a thought as sticky and glamorous as New York itself but impossible to superimpose on this boulevard of green corporate lawns, Sixty-first Street. I remembered my green bag with my clothes in it, still down in intensive care's waiting area where I had dropped it, rattled.

"You know," Lydie suddenly said, "Adrienne brought this upon herself."

I pretended not to have heard her. Sometimes people, after they emerge from a particularly intense and confined situation, have to talk things out to themselves first, before attempting polite conversation.

But Lydie kept looking at me. "What do you have in your sack?" she asked.

I still had the necktie sack in my hands. I edged out the tie, to show her the fabric. "For Adrienne, actually."

Lydie was looking not at the tie, but at the sack. She chuckled. She kept her eyes on the road. "You didn't buy that in Tulsa."

"No. No. I got it at JFK."

"You're coming from New York?"

"Yes. Chase emailed me." Which was an untruth: Chase emailed the listserv. "Is he around?"

"Not as yet."

"What about Edith?"

"Who?"

"Edith Altman?"

"I don't know who that is."

Lydie seemed thoughtful, with both hands clinging to the top of her steering wheel. "And did you come all this way just to see us?"

"Oh, well, I haven't been home in years, so. It made sense. And at Kennedy I just grabbed this—I thought it might cheer her up, actually."

She smiled. "You probably shouldn't have gone to so much trouble."

"It's no trouble."

"You came all this way."

"Well, I love Tulsa. I—can visit my parents while I'm here," I lied.

Lydie looked at me slyly and returned to her driving. And then, after a second, she again mentioned that Adrienne "had this coming."

144

"I haven't really been in touch with her," I said.

"But you know how she acts."

"I heard that she was riding a motorcycle at the time."

"But you *know* her."

"Yes," I said. "I definitely do."

"She's been asking for this ever since she was fourteen."

"You mean, because she got a motorcycle when she was fourteen?"

Lydie held her cigarette one inch in front of her face, as if she was about to jab it forward. "Jim, right? A lot of young people have motorcycles, Jim. But that doesn't make them the same as Adrienne."

"You know me?"

"Yes."

"I'm sorry I didn't introduce myself."

"That's all right."

"Did you recognize me just now?" We were pulling into the McDonald's.

"Well, no one else brought her a *present,* Jim. I remember you. I pay more attention to Adrienne than people think. You were the only one of Adrienne's friends who was ever going to amount to much. Which I think is why she was so taken with you. But we have to go in. I don't do drive-thrus."

At the cash registers, Lydie and I split up to game the two shortest lines. Small children, brought here by their mothers for the high hour of their pre-kindergarten lives, stood by at random, studying the current display of Happy Meal favors or curling up in the booths, waiting on their food. I used to be brought to this McDonald's. The boy nearest me windmilled his arms. On the way today, I had taken an interest in the corporate signs embedded in the streetside hills, OG&E, HILTI, PENNWELL: corporate marquees that when I was a new reader had seemed tediously vague.

Lydie paid. I was handed our food, two grease-bottomed sacks to carry to the car. "Make sure they got the order right." While I was bent over in my seat rummaging in the sacks, Lydie asked me to tell her what all I had done since dating Adrienne. She sat there, not starting the car.

I told her I had completed undergrad, making friends with all the professors, who packed me off to New York with letters of recommendation. About the magazine she wanted to hear more. I told her how much I got paid. "I'm technically freelance, which makes no sense: I'm expected to go there every day and sit at a desk. But that's how things work nowadays." I thought Lydie would be interested in this. "Outside of finance, almost nobody I know from college landed jobs with benefits. I actually can't even think of one person right now, sitting here."

"But you're lucky. That's a very prestigious job."

"Which is why I can't leave it. Right?"

She lit another cigarette and appeared to be thinking, so I decided to start in on the fries.

I tried to hold a fry in my lips, like it was a cigarette. I sucked on it for a while and then it started to taste like a potato, for once. The smoke from her cigarette was drawing out my window, a dense tendril right in front of me, and I chopped at it with a fry. The smoke fell apart; some of it floated down and got mixed with the gold dust on my fries.

"Should we go?"

In answer, she took another long, contemplative puff. The pale cake of her foundation glistened in the heat. "I was pleased when Adrienne started dating you," she said. "I thought: Oh—I've underestimated her! She's going to grow up now, she'll go to college."

"Well she was too smart for that. She wouldn't have been Adrienne if she'd gone to college."

Lydie smiled. "That's not fair to Adrienne."

I took a fry out of my mouth. I wanted to proceed like a plausible adult, if I could.

"College would have changed everything," Lydie said—leveling out her hand. "Everything."

"But you can't pretend that the accident is because Adrienne didn't have a college degree."

"Yes, I'm sorry Jim. But it is actually. That's actually how life works. You go up or you go down." Lydie took a puff of her cigarette, and then she continued in a weary voice. "Her accident is the logical result of Adrienne's career. You're upset. But you have to realize, I've been dealing with Adrienne ever since she was a little girl. To me, you know, I've been watching this wreck in slow motion."

She was powerful, this lady. With her deft gesticulations she had the steely pace of a practiced public speaker. As she talked, she pressed her mane back against her headrest; she seemed to grow larger and larger in her seat.

She started up the car.

I said, "Coming here that summer and dating Adrienne was one of the smartest things I ever did."

"But you didn't stay."

"No. No, I wasn't brave enough, actually."

"But you wish you had?"

I looked at the brown fence of the McDonald's. "Sometimes I do."

She was twisted around to look behind her, backing out. "Jim," she said, "you're going to be happy in life. And she's not. That's all you can really say, and it's all you need to know."

I liked Lydie, enough to fight with her. Obviously she didn't get her niece. It was adolescent to say so. But if Lydie was going to judge what happened to Adrienne so permanently tragic I could at least establish how worthwhile in the first place Adrienne was. Adrienne was great. Great not as a raw estimate of worth but as a specific virtue: greatness. Lydie, a woman of means and connections, might have appreciated what I meant: something about Adrienne's self-possession, her boldness. Adrienne taught us how to *use time*. But then again Lydie may not have realized how much time someone like me, with my special little record of achievement, had wasted.

The beginning of time say is middle school. A huge blasted cratered wasteland of an area. For me literally a wide windswept derelict parking lot, where for three years I waited every morning for the bus. I found myself at the bus stop each morning as if newly created, solitary, blinking in the darkness. The material of the backpack was cold and plastic, my jeans were cold, my socks felt cottony and coarsely knit. The other kids waited under an awning at one end of a long, stadium-sized parking lot: every morning I was dropped off at the opposite end, and started across. I didn't romanticize it, but trudged across, with neither presence of mind nor interest. The winter wind built up across the lot and opened up the sky. I kept my head down: I studied the tar, the differently flaked patches. Cars would well up at the light behind me, and then I would hear them drain away.

It was the most muted time in my life, and everything that I then expected—sex, music, some kind of heroism—seemed to jostle behind it like a curtain. I found nothing to say to my schoolmates. Nor they to me. Our awning belonged to an abandoned movie theater; we stood spaced out one person to each pole. Eventually I made friends with Jamie Livingstone, and we two started to stand at the same pole. We weren't very *good* friends: Jamie bobbed his head in his headphones. I guess he tried to stay upbeat, but we didn't talk much, and I never knew what was going on in his life, though we were friends for years. I remember that his T-shirts were all made of cheap heavyweight material and hung stiffly from his shoulders. For a while he wore a string necklace with a yin-yang symbol on it, but I never asked him about it.

Each day, when the school bus appeared at the far intersection, we all filed out from under the awning and lined up on the curbside grass. We squinted to confirm the bus number, 286, stenciled above the bus's front window; and in the event that a strange bus stopped we stood there to parley with it, like members of a little village. We didn't get on without checking. It was our experience that substitute bus drivers often went sailing off course and dragged our schedules to pieces. Then we arrived at school late and had to go into the office and demand clemency. We would excoriate the bus driver in front of the assistant principal. Jamie was not a natural leader, but in these situations, and at the bus stop, he often was our spokesman. He seemed to know what his rights were. He was good at talking to bus drivers.

He took a worried interest in me, quizzing me about bands, and you could see in this and in other things the influence of his parents, and what they took seriously. Jamie could be almost grim: Have you heard of such-and-such band? And do you like them? I had not heard of, in most cases. My parents did not teach me such things. To know already, as Jamie did, would have been to enter life somehow tutored. Jamie would hand over the CDs he lent me as soon as I stepped under the awning, taking the jewel case quickly from his bag, expecting me to slip it into mine. I always wanted to take some time to study the cover. Jamie would toss his hair out of his eyes impatiently. Only when I got my own private seat on the bus could I take the CD out and read the lyrics. Once we got to school Jamie and I seldom talked together. I think he had a hard time. Was I ever disloyal to him? Of course.

Way up in the penthouse, though, with Adrienne Booker, I sometimes thought of Jamie. I wondered what that guy was doing. There had never been much to say, or to remember: being the so-called fag patrol. What Jamie and I had experienced in middle school was at best a kind of numbness. But it was different than the storied humiliation of boys' schools—oh, we might have loved that. We read books about stuff like that—or about dragons and sorcery—and held them up over our eyes so we wouldn't have to look at our pretty classmates.

When Adrienne Booker waggled out of her skirt, she seemed so straight, like an arrow lodged forever in her own layer of reality. She paced across the room so I would have to watch: up on tiptoe she leaned towards me and smiled and let her khaki skirt fall. She was just having fun. She didn't know, like I did, how unlikely she was. Perhaps this was why our relationship failed: that I never told her how much I relished the irony. That there was an angle on our love I could share only with someone like Jamie Livingstone. When Adrienne sat Indian-style across from me and said first we had to stare at each other for five minutes as a prerequisite to touching, I knew then that the fog of boyhood would never again touch my brain. She was the most palpable person I had ever met. Her body was so much heavier than it looked, there was always so much of it lengthwise. I sometimes thought I might get her sitting partway up on a pillow so that she extended in three dimensions like a jack. She would simply undo my pants, or would stand up in the bed and tear my shirt off over my head. I remember she always tried to undress me first. Except in the mornings, when we were blessed with a kind of neoclassical convenience, being already naked: We often woke up talking. A clarity I've never had with anyone else. Adrienne always made me speak precisely, and even reviewed me: Was that the lintel over there, or the doorjamb? I was expected to put a word to my feelings, to explain and explain. I had told her I was a poet, after all. It had been her way of encouraging me; she tried to get out of my way so I could verbalize. I preferred to touch her. In bed it was limb limb, the pleasure of the awkwardness of her two long legs, trying to steer them down and upside down was more rapid and communicative than anything she would ever want me to repeat afterwards. I squeezed, to emphasize: my happiness was much more than I could say.

What about someone like Jamie? He could drive down 169 to the movies, or buy a CD at Best Buy. He could complain about what they played on the radio. He never heard about local bands, and he seldom had cause to go downtown. He could find some friends, presumably, but without resources—without venues—all they could do was compare notes and talk about foreign movies. Like spies who had heard rumors of the world.

Jamie was left out. And I almost had been too. Adrienne lived in a certain world, and if its borders did not exactly correspond to downtown, they nonetheless existed, and I wanted to stomp my foot on that border and declare, This division exists. I have crossed it.

So when Lydie compelled me to defend Adrienne, saying that Adrienne should have gone to college and that that would have been saving herself, and I was tempted to say in response how much Adrienne's glamour meant to me, how brinkmanlike it was and fierce, I desisted only because I despaired of explaining. You cannot seriously say that you love someone because they are cool or argue about "being cool" as if it was a value—one that trumps education. It isn't done.

Lydie assumed that people like me merely walked up a ramp into her proximity, happy to rise. But I did it for the girls. Nothing Lydie assumed—about college, about New York, about New York magazines—accounted for the romanticism that brought it all up so sharp to my senses. I had whetted my own appetite. Lydie could never fathom that period of years when I wasn't even hungry yet and was just trudging through, learning band trivia from Jamie—who now apparently had a bone disease. And was in a hospital himself, elsewhere in this city. Another irony just for me. The real world was bestowing its rewards, at least on those who had stayed in Tulsa. But Adrienne remained a thing in my head to grip, a staff and a standard. Someone to swim for, a hero.

3

Rod met us in the lobby. "Her friends are with her," he explained. I made an effort to finish my hamburger. Dashing upstairs I almost tripped, but once I reached the sixth floor I veered past Adrienne's door (I heard their voices) and walked a loop through the ward.

I had been thinking about calling my parents. I would proudly tell them I was back in Tulsa. Though I wouldn't be able to tell them why: they would think it crazy that I had come back after five years to tend to this particular girlfriend. There was a window bay down the corridor, and I could picture myself standing there calling them, looking out over South Tulsa in the direction of Texas. But what would it even mean to my parents, to hear that I was back in Tulsa? It would seem like a bitter act. As if I resented them leaving here. Was that the case? I wondered.

Neurology had its own good-sized lounge, with a TV and an array of couches, and I decided to wait there. Among the ill-slept families sitting through the painful afternoon I observed a young man talking on the phone, sitting with his ankles crossed, in cargo pants. It sounded like he was on the phone with his wife: ". . . nope, nope. Tell them. Mmhm. For supper."

And then I heard him mention Adrienne.

"Are you friends with that girl in there?" I asked, sitting down next to him as soon as he hung up.

"I'm sorry?"

"Her—I guess paralysis?" I said. "It's terrible."

"Oh, she's going to be okay. *They're goin' to do a surgery in the mornin'.*" He said it in a croaky, singsong voice—as if it was *a hangin' in the mornin'.*

I pulled my pants fabric straight on my lap. "Yeah, that's what I heard."

His name was Nic. He was a natural gossip. He told me that Adrienne had been up at Bartlesville on the night of the accident. That explained why she ended up out here by the highway, rather than at one of the midtown hospitals.

Nic worked in a reference to Albert's barn as "our friend's personal recording studio."

"Right. So she was recording?"

No. She was drinking. And afterwards, when she came out to get on her motorcycle, young Nic was there on the patio. He told her not to drive. He was high—but he could see she wasn't fit to drive. He had been sitting out there reading the stars, that night. Mars was out. "I thought that would get through to her."

As Nic talked, a fit young woman exiting the elevator walked past in the direction of Adrienne's room.

I thought it was Kim Wheel—a grown-up Kim Wheel. From that point on, half my attention was down the hall.

"So you know Adrienne pretty well?" I casually asked.

Nic shrugged.

"She's hard to know," I offered.

"Wait—you know her?"

"Well yeah."

"I was under the impression that you didn't know her."

He was almost offended. I enjoyed the moment. But I asked him to go on, to tell me what had happened.

He obliged: Adrienne wrecked on Albert's own private drive.

"Was it paved? I don't remember."

He cut his eyes at me. "Uh, Albert had it redone. That's the thing. He shortened it, and got the turnoff from the highway changed. So she went straight when she should have turned."

"She drove straight off the road?"

"Yes sir."

"Oh, God." It pained me that Adrienne had made such a definite mistake. I had been assigning the fault to another car, some moron behind a long hood.

"On a motorcycle," Nic said, "when you know you're going too fast into a turn, you have to make a decision. You either commit, and lean into the turn that much harder, or you straighten up. The key with motorcycles is you've got to look into a turn, you've got to see a line through the turn. If you straighten up though you do have maximum braking potential, and that's what Adrienne may have been thinking. But if she'd really laid the bike down . . ."

She would not have gone flying through the air. He went on about technical details, but what moved me was the fact she'd been following the old road. Adrienne had been on a kind of autopilot in her head.

"So the crash was technically off-road," Nic concluded. "She hit an old tree stump and flipped her vehicle." I bent my wrist forward as it was explained to me, flattening the back of my hand on the table in front of us so that my elbow popped forward: Adrienne flew into the air.

Nic had actually been down there before work this morning, to look for skid marks. I was impressed.

"There weren't any marks?"

"No. Anyway, if she had braked, I would have heard it."

"You were close enough?"

"I was the one who called the ambulance. She was only fifty yards down the drive. I heard a crash, and started running. Once I saw the vehicle I had my phone out."

I wished I had been with him, running in the dark. I stared. "Thank you," I said.

He looked at me.

"Was she wearing a helmet?" I asked.

"Adrienne? That's not really her style."

"No. I guess not." I was stung.

Those from Adrienne's room were now flushed out. I looked for Edith. The whole group was mostly strangers— but Jenny Mayhew walked at their head—and never let a

Sunday school teacher tell you otherwise, it is often a great thing to have slept with a person. I found the courage to rise from my chair and greet her. And here was Kim Wheel, the announcements reader. She stopped in her tracks. "Jim Praley."

Six or seven years out of high school, Kim and I no longer knew how to rate each other. I guess we were friends, slightly. She was shaking my hand quite sympathetically; she was skinnier than she used to be. She had been getting sun, I observed. The skin on her collarbones was spotted.

She and Jenny both sat down.

In chaos, a few polite questions were asked: Kim was applying to medical school next year, and for now was getting a premed certificate at the OU extension campus. And Jenny was getting her bachelor's—Jenny hadn't aged at all. Her red mouth smacked, her eyes forever evaluated and stared, amazed. She flicked her hair off her shoulders every time she was about to speak. But her level speech, which had sounded seriously childish when she was fifteen, fit her now, and seemed earned.

I explained that I had gotten the news by email, and had simply decided to come.

Kim gazed at me. "You flew here? Wow."

"I'm a romantic fool." I bit my lip and drummed my fingers on the chair's plastic armrests.

"You're sweet," said Kim.

Jenny crossed her legs, and then Kim crossed her legs as well, the two girls crossing them in the same direction.

I turned to Nic.

"You seem to know everybody," he said.

"Jim was Adrienne's boyfriend," said Jenny.

I glanced at Kim. But Kim apparently knew all about Adrienne and me. I thought I might be blushing, but I wasn't.

Nic asked when it was that I had dated Adrienne. "During the Clinton administration," I said. I looked up. "I'm—it's such a privilege to come back," I said.

Our conversation patrolled the city, and the women told me about new developments, the artificial islands built in the Arkansas River, and the roller coaster that got torn down last year—but I couldn't figure out whether Kim and Jenny knew each other well, or if these shared points of reference were the only stuff we could talk about. "I have to admit I'm aching a little bit to go downtown or something," I said. "In New York I'm always, like, take me back to the Blumont."

"That place blows," said Jenny. "They fired all the old bartenders."

I reached out. "How is Chase, though—I guess he's not here?"

"He's a film editor." Jenny looked to Nic for confirmation.

"He's only an assistant," said Nic. "They do a lot of big shitty action movies."

"So he's not around much?"

Jenny raised her eyebrows. "Well, I think he keeps track of Adrienne."

"What do you mean?"

"You knew she moved to L.A.?"

"Oh."

Jenny shied her knee into the air, as if startled.

Kim leaned in and touched Jenny's thigh. "Adrienne was only in town visiting, is that right?"

Jenny: "Yeah. I hadn't seen her since Christmas."

"Strange she didn't visit more often," I interjected, trying to keep my voice level. "It must have been different, in a new city."

"It's actually really healthy for her, I think," said Jenny.

"And Edith Altman has helped her a lot, hasn't she?" asked Kim.

"That's where Edith is?"

"She's a casting agent," said Jenny.

"Adrienne was doing movies?"

"No."

Kim grabbed my knee. "Have you heard the album?"

"The one from back then?"

Everyone looked at me in confusion.

"She was going to make an album with Albert Dooney?"

Kim looked to Jenny for backup. "This was her first album. Just last winter. It's been really well received."

Nic concurred, vaguely.

My dominant feeling was one of losing control. There ought to be something I could say, a story I could tell, to make them understand how close she had been to me. But she had moved. In my agitation, I couldn't even raise my eyes to look at the others, and the center of the conversation was now, without anyone having said anything, on my distress. "I'm just thinking . . ." I tried. They waited. "What you said, Nic, about her not

161

wearing a helmet." I reached my fingers out, from where I sat crumpled in my seat, and traced a zigzag through the air. "She's still asleep?"

Tulsa belongs to the East. It belongs to the forest of broadleaf trees that unrolls off the backside of the Appalachians and carpets the South. Farther than Tulsa the trees thin, and then you get the Oklahoma of famous photographs, the flats of silver gelatin spreading out, in the Dust Bowl. The Okies go to California. Tulsa is some degree back off that, up from the plains. It's the endpoint of a different migration: of civilized tribes forced to leave farms in Georgia and in Florida. Who walked all the way here. And who then had this area to themselves, for a time.

I watched Adrienne in her bed, her chest rising and falling, and I saw her old dresses, puffing in the wind. I remembered Tulsa. We preferred the streets at noon, at their emptiest. Not like California. I disliked the idea of California. I pictured Adrienne in L.A. standing at the rail of that famous observatory, posing. It was unpleasant to think of Adrienne as anything other than in control, in her own mind. To move to a city—as I well knew—you have to be ready to almost degrade yourself with eagerness. You have to be ready to show up at thousands of events and parties and not even know really whether you're invited. I didn't think Adrienne would be very good at that. The Adrienne I knew stood at her easel, her bottom in her pants. She could stand still for an hour at a time.

Lydie didn't understand why I was so upset. "She was young and single, Jim, and she moved to California."

I had assumed I would somehow know if Adrienne ever moved—I really did feel I would have contacted her, had I known she had left Tulsa. She should have come East though, if she was going to relocate. But she shouldn't have moved at all. Adrienne never traveled. Which was part of what made her so attractive. That she was sufficient unto herself. Maybe Lydie was half right: something had gone wrong. Maybe the accident was somehow a testament to how far off course Adrienne had got. And Adrienne had been depressed—but Adrienne wasn't allowed to get depressed.

Jenny found me in a corner, staring into space. She asked me if I wanted to go up to the roof.

I didn't know you could go up there. I followed Jenny up the emergency stairwell and out a big push-bar door into the night air.

She walked quickly across the gravel. "This is nice, right?!"

It was a relief. The door's security light illuminated the near roof, but the rest was blackness, tabling out over the city lights. Jenny was wearing short shorts, and the backs of her legs flashed like bowling pins as she hurried out of the light. She walked straight toward the best view: the faraway skyscrapers stood out in three dimensions, while the intervening neighborhoods lay flat, like a bed of glittering soil. I thought how the Tulsa skyscrapers were more timid and beautifully protuberant than New York's. "The city looks great," I said. But Jenny wasn't listening. She was scraping around for something behind the ledge's cornice. "Shit." The security lights had gone out. But Jenny stood up and flourished a bottle. "For dark times," she said. Her voice was husky. I think she felt self-conscious, surprising me with a bottle of whiskey.

At our backs an exhaust vent suddenly let go a plume of steam, and we had to move. I handed the bottle back to Jenny, and she led the way, trailing along the lip of the roof. She was short in front of me. Her brown hair, the back of her head, and her long-sleeved jacket were all lost to the night, and I followed the glint of the bottle dangling down next to her bare legs. "It's wonderful about the whiskey," I said.

"We planted it last night," she explained. "We're here for the long haul."

By "we" I didn't know who she meant, the kids downstairs in collective—or did she mean to imply that a more select posse was lately manifest: Jenny and one or two other kids, who were now running things? I had drifted through the late afternoon and evening among these groups, in the waiting lounge. I had been steeled for rejection—I thought of myself as a prodigal son, unlooked-for, probably resented. I made sure to greet Adrienne's new friends with a mild, statesmanlike smile. I tried a handshake when I could. But none of them cared who I was. The world wasn't as coherent as I had remembered. They didn't even know each other, lots of them. Maybe it all fell apart, after Adrienne went to L.A. I had half imagined giving a speech to explain myself. But there was no occasion. Lydie was the only person who recognized how weird it was of me, to have come.

"Lydie asked me to sit up with Rod tonight," I said,

"in Adrienne's room. So I'll have to be back downstairs in an hour."

"That's cool," Jenny said. On the way up here she had snatched a hospital blanket off a cart, and now she spread it out before us so we could sit on the gravel at the edge of the roof.

Jenny and I were so funny that time we hooked up and snuck into the woods at Bartlesville. We crossed the cabin's yard with huge blankets heaped on our heads, like disguises—even though it was already broad morning. It was some gesture at secrecy—to pretend what we were doing was illicit. Yet my thought at the time had been not that I was betraying Adrienne, but that I was doing something to impress her. It was the sort of thing that Adrienne taught me. I wasn't sure the kids here at the hospital got it. Be tough. Have some fun. Do the math. There is a moral obligation to do what you want. Don't spare yourself out of a sentimental sense of etiquette.

I took a drink of whiskey and handed it back to Jenny. I could make out the contour of Jenny's throat as she swallowed. She wiped her mouth. "So how's New York?" she asked. "That's what we should be talking about."

"I mean. It's a great city. But you have to have a lot of money."

"Adrienne's like that about L.A. too, like all blasé: L.A. sucks."

I didn't like this topic. "Would you ever move, like that?"

"I'm going to go to New York actually, after college."

I could see Jenny in New York. Sometimes my

165

friends and I arrived at parties where I had little idea how we had been invited, but we entered and asserted our rights, and took beer out of the refrigerator. And at these parties where we knew absolutely no one, where the girls had dressed up, and the apartment was hung with posters we had all seen around, we heard their boys grumbling—as if it was not just their apartment they could kick us out of, but New York itself. It was painfully obvious how many parallel worlds us kids in New York were renting. We went into these parties and tried to steal the girls. And when that worked it was simple. But when a nice girl hesitated, if you started to feel sorry for her, that was when you could see: where she had come from, and where she was trying to go.

She had found this vintage dress, and her bookcase was full of books. And her boys were probably very good boys. To some extent she was living the dream. And it was to just that extent that I wished her absolutely the best, and went home feeling sorry for her and for myself and for every kid in the city.

"You should go to New York," I told Jenny.

Jenny had lit a cigarette. "So New York and not L.A.?"

"Do you remember the time Adrienne cut off her ponytail?" Once, toward the end of that summer, Adrienne had cut off her ponytail onstage, while singing. She whipped it away so it came apart like a pack of spaghetti over our heads. She had hair-sprayed it before, so it was stiff.

Jenny was in no mood to reminisce. People like

Adrienne and me would go on trying to be artists, until it was too late, and kids like Jenny would long since have accepted the reality of their lives. Chase would be a real artist. Edith was Edith. But Jenny would grow up and be able to sit in judgment of us all, that I knew. And the gravel on the roof was still quite warm, heated through all day, and its wild tinny smell came up to me now in the dark. I had to take advantage of this moment with Jenny. I should tell her a secret or something. But what are you supposed to do in life? Are you supposed to sleep with everyone you meet?

"I wish she hadn't moved," I said.

Jenny was sitting with her legs tucked under her, like a shepherdess.

"You and I are alike," I told her. "We do things like going to college, going to big cities. We need that sort of stuff."

"Most people," Jenny said, "leave."

"But Adrienne stayed here for what, how many years after she dropped out of high school, before she left? I know I'm sentimental about Tulsa. But Adrienne wasn't even thinking about it. She just looped in her own loops." I did my finger in a circle, and went on: "She painted when she wanted to paint. I was glad somebody in the world was living like that." I glanced at Jenny. "Of course it was only possible because of her family."

"Did you always know them?"

"I met Lydie once that summer. But that's it." I was still waiting to hear what Jenny thought about what I had said.

"Adrienne never really talked about her family much."

"Right. The fantasy we all have of Adrienne is that she's quintessentially parentless."

"I wish she was."

"But she's like Lydie. Definitely more than she would admit."

"I heard that Lydie is going to like give Adrienne to some doctors in Virginia for some medical experiment?"

"Uh, the UVA trial is one of lots of options Lydie is exploring. She has to do something. And the experiments are a really expedient way of getting Adrienne admitted to a selective rehab program." I was pulling rank on this. Though I liked the idea that the kids were making up paranoid conspiracy theories.

"But like Rod," Jenny persisted. "Don't you think it's strange that, after staying away for *so long,* he comes now? Like Nic said: you know Rod's worried about what'll she say to him when she wakes up."

I stared at Jenny and grinned. "Rod and I both," I said, "are supposed to sit up with Adrienne tonight. And maybe she'll wake up." I took another long drink from the bottle. Jenny was quiet.

"Do you think Adrienne'll be all right?" I asked.

"If the doctors say so, I guess." Jenny said this weakly.

"Lydie told me that the bowel function might be permanently damaged."

Jenny said nothing.

"But what is that about?" I asked.

Jenny didn't want to discuss it.

I looked at Jenny, or tried to look at her, in the dark. "I hate to think about it," I said.

Jenny might reach out, Jenny might say something like, You love her very much, don't you?

But Jenny wouldn't say anything of the kind. "I'm getting drunk," she said. "I should go home soon."

It had been kind, very kind of her, to take me up here. We got up, and folded the hospital blanket. The air was still warm—hot, even, like there might be lightning. "I did really used to love her," I said. I was making this confession as if to compensate Jenny somehow, as if she needed to have some takeaway from this tête-à-tête.

So I came to Rod with liquor on my breath. "Am I late?" I asked. I checked Adrienne's face. There was a bruise that I monitored, and since that afternoon it had already turned from black to yellow.

Rod was looking at me strangely.

"Lydie told me to be here at eleven," I said.

"Did she?"

"She did."

"That's funny." Rod leaned forward like a fat man, with his hands on his knees. "I told her I would be here."

"Well she said that I should help you."

He seemed puzzled for a second, and then he squeezed up his eyes. "Jesus."

I hadn't really thought this through: Lydie was using me like a pawn. I was here as her agent. But I asked Rod to let me stay anyway; I had all my baggage here already, I told him.

"Make yourself at home."

While I was getting seated he briefed me on the medical situation. He explained the latest issue: that when they bolted a rod to Adrienne's spine it would give her a very slight stoop, five degrees or so. This would be permanent, a part of tomorrow morning's stabilization surgery.

"Five degrees seems like a lot," I said. I didn't want to hurt his feelings—but he was already on to all the technical aspects anyway, how the metal would react with the tissue. He very much laid it out for me—as if he was the doctor, and *I* was the patient's father.

"I thought they were just going to staple it."

He shook his head fiercely.

With Rod in front of me, with his snow-white beard and his raw blushing neck, I could begin to reconstruct why Adrienne, age twelve, had deigned not to follow him East. I didn't exactly blame him for not being a father to her; indeed he did not seem to *be* a father. He was innocent of that. I felt bad about his not knowing what to say, and his resultant sentimentality—like when he said, "That's really a tribute," about my coming here. If he was a little repetitive about Adrienne's spinal cord and the science, that was understandable. Perhaps he would open up as the night wore on.

I got us some of the nurses' coffee. And then, as will happen late at night, we made a plan to get some food. I told Rod that there was a barbeque place with twenty-four-hour delivery. I knew it from "the old days," I alluded, hoping to intrigue him. I had practically lived in this man's rooms, in the penthouse. "Are you staying at the Booker?" I asked.

No, he said, the Booker gave him the creeps. Rod seemed to think that his family's business, Booker Petroleum, was evil. I tried again: Did he ever consider moving back to Tulsa at all? I thought Rod and I could have in common a certain flavor of regret. In a very softball way, we were both self-exiled. But Rod misunderstood. He started to supply me with all the different reasons why I was *right* to have left our shared hometown. "But then sometimes you want fish," he said. He granted that local barbeque was pretty good: "Good, but not the best. And if you want sushi? God help you." I didn't have the heart to tell Rod that decent-enough sushi was widely available in Tulsa. "Did you ever try to vote for anyone in this town?" Rod asked. "It's like beating your head against the wall. You might as well vote Communist as vote Democrat for President."

When the barbeque came, we ate silently, side by side.

Rod was basically like Albert. Both were oil babies, who abdicated their place in the adult world and tried in vain to justify themselves. They belittled the city—they were especially harsh about its lack of culture. Even growing up, I knew people like this, men and women— though from the middle class—whose chief consolation in life was cynicism—we all did it. Because the city of Tulsa was easy to put down. In New York, I reflected, this was less common. There are lots of ways to be cynical about New York, but it's rather uncommon to act too good for it. But in Tulsa—we were the worst. Us kids.

It was not until I interviewed for college, and visited local alumni from various out-of-state universities in their homes, that I realized Tulsa actually had leaders— people like Lydie, people who believed in it and who got business done. For my interviews I went in succession to a gray house, a red house, a blue house. Inside I found a small-time CEO, a local dean, a lawyer. At the gray house, the CEO took me into his three-car garage and showed me his Corvette collection: He was the first person in years who told me to my face that being smart wasn't good enough. I should play sports too. The man in the red house had the best chair for me, set in an alcove with books on either side as if to buttress me; he sat in a hard chair out in the open and let me volley at him. The man in the blue house, by contrast, was frankly impatient. If I hadn't read as much as him, then too bad. Nonetheless, I left his house that night as I had left the others, starstruck, preoccupied of course with my chances to go East, but also gazing into the night sky, wondering just what powers constellated themselves un-dreamt-of in Tulsa. Growing up in Tulsa, watching the nightly news, you never would have guessed that power was conducted by these calm, well-installed individuals, that Tulsa was studded with them. It flattered me just to know they existed.

Surely these men who had interviewed me in the nineties had also gone to the same Tulsa galas where Rod would have shown up, in his sunglasses probably, a goofball in the sixties. Surely Rod knew them, knew their names, knew them from years-ago parties, had gone to the same one or two local private schools with them, and remembered them as you do, haunted by an adolescent memory, a dirty joke that was whispered in your ear when you were too young. There must have been parties, weddings, before I was born, when all these people were young men. And I could well imagine Rod avoiding the guys who were really smart—the guys who were to impress me so much, decades later. Rod just went back to the drinks table. Rod moved to Rhode Island, and judged the world from there. From the beach. Because Rod hadn't played the power games that were his class prerogative, his politics were bullshit. That was what I thought.

We were asleep already in our chairs—or I thought we were—when another person came into the room. I assumed it was a nurse. "Everyone else is gone," she said, as if to explain herself, and sat down. It was Chase Fitzpatrick's mother. Her name was Carrie: I had seen her in the lounge earlier that evening, and we had been quickly introduced. I had remembered her from the time I rang the Fitzpatricks' doorbell and Carrie answered, and I gave her the collage-book I had made for Adrienne. I was astonished that Carrie was still here, that she came in now. And she sat down just as if she was going to stay all night. She adjusted her skirt in the chair. "Adrienne's such a special girl," she said. She was gazing at the patient.

Carrie had good bones, and bangs cut across her forehead, but vicious crow's-feet that she obviously tried to cover up but could not. She was probably about forty-five. Her manner was all politeness, and yet she did not seem to take into account that we had been sitting here, with our take-out containers as yet undiscarded and smelling, that for untold minutes now we had been sitting in an easy, ursine silence.

"Chase is trying to get her a job, you know, Rod. But she's too busy singing. All our children are so busy! But she could do anything, Rod. Even in a wheelchair. You know her. Adrienne could do absolutely anything."

Carrie couldn't quite figure out how I fit in. "Chase wanted me to say hello to everybody," she said to me, tentatively. "He wishes he could be here. But they're wrapping their movie."

She talked so much I couldn't concentrate on what she was saying; I grew actively afraid she would wake Adrienne—I resented Carrie coming in here. I felt Rod and I each had a claim to Adrienne's bedside—in different ways our two voices belonged in Adrienne's psychic space. But Carrie spoiled it; she was as silly as us, but somehow more generic, or realistic. Trying to be a mom like she was.

"If you two want to go lie down on the couches and get some sleep, I can wait in here," she told us. But as soon as she said that her phone rang. I didn't know who it was—some other thin middle-aged woman, awake on antidepressants in the middle of the night. Carrie was telling this woman all about Adrienne's condition: the surgery tomorrow morning, how it was just going to be preliminary, to stabilize Adrienne, and how Adrienne would have to fight, and how there would be physical therapy. And then she got into Adrienne's whole backstory. "No. Huh-uh. No college. She never finished high school. Uh-huh. Uh-huh. But she's a good girl. She's neat. Yeah. Ever since they were little. Preschool. But she's had lots of problems . . ."

I rose and laid my hand on Carrie's shoulder. She didn't flinch, she accepted my touch naturally, like it was a comfort. She didn't stop her conversation. The silk of her blouse turned warm under my touch and finally I crouched down, I tried to be kind: "Rod and I want to stay with the patient tonight, I think. I think we'll try to sleep."

Carrie put her hand over the receiver. "Okay."

Maybe I imagined it, maybe I was dizzy with fatigue, but it was like I had to stare her down then, squatting by her side, getting through to her the idea that she had to leave.

"Okay," she said. "You need my phone number though."

She had her phone back on her ear as she dictated me the number, making the poor other woman sit through it while she gave me instructions. Finally she left, and we could hear her resume her conversation, fading down the hall: "Hey there. Yeah, they're okay, I think they're going to be okay."

Rod was smiling—at my valor, or at my foolish territorial pride.

"She's a tough case," he said.

I spent much of that night listening to Rod snore. I had never been a snorer, so far as I knew—I compared Rod, a week ago, him snoring alone in Rhode Island, with me, probably silent as a fish, in Brooklyn.

4

Adrienne's stabilizing surgery was successful. Her neck was secured, and her thoracic vertebra was stapled. I sat it out all morning with everyone else.

I was talking to Kim Wheel.

"There was once this NHS thing, planting trees. You won't remember, but we were all carpooling. I was in your car. And there was a beer bottle rolling around on the floor mats." I looked at Kim.

She looked at me. She didn't get it.

I raised my hands, to signal my innocence. "There was a beer bottle touching my leg!"

Kim laughed.

"I was there in your backseat with my legs in this crazy position the whole time, to keep from touching it." I had hiked my feet up in the air and was about to fall out of the waiting lounge chair. People were looking.

Kim was telling me how she and Adrienne became friends. They had taken the same yoga class, as it happened, prior to Adrienne's move West.

"It must have been me who mentioned your name. We would talk about Franklin. But when I mentioned you it was a big deal. Adrienne got all serious."

Kim bugged her eyes out. She was trying to do Adrienne's stone-cold, divine stare.

I nodded, to encourage Kim. "I imagine Adrienne's good at yoga," I offered. Kim seemed tempted to take this wickedly and I interjected, "She has had such great powers of concentration."

"Tell me stories," said Kim.

I stared.

Kim's eyes twinkled.

"Well, you know—I don't know what kind of time you spent with her, but she could stand all day in front of her work, meditating."

Kim kept smiling. "She said you taught her art history."

I gestured roughly. "I didn't teach her anything."

"We always used to get smoothies," Kim said, "after yoga. It made us hungry—everybody else in the class was moms. It was funny for me because I always thought, Adrienne Booker, what a mystery, she dropped out. And I heard things about her, you know. But then here the two of us were, at Salad Alley. And that she dated you."

I was tired. I had barely slept the night before, and had been riding on adrenaline this morning, all the well-wishers coming into the waiting lounge for Adrienne's surgery and me there already, like a host. I had tried to ignore the headache brightness of the waiting lounge lights.

"She said she hadn't heard from you in years."

"She said that?"

Kim's voice deliberately softened. "Why did you never come back?"

I felt lost, drifting away for a second. "I don't know." I crossed my legs. "I mean, there are rules, aren't there? After a certain amount of time you can't get back in touch anymore."

Kim slapped the plastic couch where she was sitting with some resolve. "After this I'm on my way to see Jamie Livingstone."

"Oh?"

"You have to come, Jim. You were friends, weren't you?"

"Well, Jamie and I rode the same bus." It seemed like another life to me. I knew he probably wouldn't want me to make any kind of overture.

But Kim was always friends with everybody, in a popular-girl kind of way. My sense of reserve seemed almost sardonic in comparison. "You should get out of the hospital for a while," she told me. I couldn't really argue with her.

Finally, the neurosurgeon came in and confronted this reef of sleepy, half-skeptical young people, sought out Rod, and informed the patient's father that the operation had gone smoothly. Adrienne "did a great job." As no one would be allowed to go in to see Adrienne for hours yet, Kim and I rose to make our exit. But Kim wouldn't take French leave, and I had to stand there like an impatient husband while she said her goodbyes.

We took separate cars. That was the way of it: always like a convoy setting out into the veldt, in Tulsa.

I pulled up alongside Kim: "Instead of the highway let's take Yale." Yale was the avenue I used to live off of, named Yale by the dirt-road, brass-banister generation that had laid Tulsa out—trying to embolden themselves, I guess, with big names. We had a Harvard Avenue too. When they were laid out, these roads cut through open prairies, but long ago they had been subdivided, graced with inexpensive split-levels: the neighborhoods still remained spacious, and it was out here that Adrienne and I had found the Hobby Lobby and the Target and the other air-conditioned big boxes that softened our afternoons, that summer. This was home. As a kid I always used to come with my dad after dinner, to fill up the car at these gas stations. It was a quiet thing to do, our stomachs full, watching evening traffic for a minute from the cool smooth concrete. I took in the fumes like sea air. Or we would go running errands on Saturdays, different places: back and forth, out onto the blacktop, downcast in the perpendicular sunlight, then back in: fueled by Coca-Cola and succored by the AC vent. I leaned my head directly on it. In our plush backseat there was an exposed joint of lubricated metal, the back bench of our minivan being collapsible, and I often wiggled my finger down between the cushions and then drew it out, to smell the grease on my finger.

I honked and pointed out my window, to signal to Kim that we should stop at the QuikTrip ahead to buy something to drink. "I want a Big-Gulp-type thing," I explained once we got out of our cars.

"When was the last time you were in town?"

"My parents moved away after that summer, so."

We stood with our straws in our mouths on the curb in front of QuikTrip, bashfully listening to an unshaven man on the pay phone behind us. He was trying to borrow money from someone, an old girlfriend, it sounded like.

"Lydie says you've been a big help."

I took that in. "Do you think Lydie felt abandoned when Adrienne left town?"

"Well. Lydie . . ." Kim looked off down the street. "She took us both out to lunch once, before Adrienne left. That's how I know Lydie. But I think that was Adrienne's farewell to her. And she invited me along."

After the surgery, Lydie had left without ceremony, rushing off to a meeting—she was about to buy a geothermal energy company in Texas. All during the surgery she and one of her lawyers, Gilbert Lee, had been going over strategy in a vacant conference room in the hospital. For a while, early in the morning, Lydie had let me sit in. I had been impressed, particularly with the lawyer's clarity of mind—and with their general air of engagement and proactive self-interest so early in the morning. In some alert corner of my mind I wondered if Oklahoma could become a leader in geothermal energies. That would be good.

After Yale, Kim and I turned left onto Twenty-first Street—the street my mother and I always took going to elementary school. I had been a transfer student, to a better district, and Kim and I were now retracing the route my mother and I had driven daily into the wealthier parts of the city. I did not think then in terms of money. These were simply the more rooted parts of Tulsa, the older parts: the parts with taller trees and hence more elaborately inflected houses—it was obvious that the two things worked by the same encouragement: age, pulling up the peaked roofs, knotting the chimneys and bulging out dormers and balconies, gnarling the ironwork—trees grew taller and the old growth spread itself out, fluxing and rising. In those days I had never even been in a two-story house before. Taken on tours snaking out from our elementary school, I was always amazed to hear that some of the houses, the very oldest ones, dated from as far back as the 1920s.

That made them more than sixty years old.

But even since then, in my short life span, Tulsa had grown older. Trees grew as they individualized. I observed that some of the newer trees, meant to dignify the newer strip malls, had since my school days lifted their bush into the sky, some bending over backwards, some like thrusting arms holding their orb aloft. Hedges, having different destinies, had grown wild and fat.

With my car already lagging behind Kim's I slowed down to rubberneck at the four-story office tower my mom and I had watched go up morning after morning in the 1980s—I hadn't known then that you could simply build a building. I thought all the buildings we were meant to have were already here, and official. The turreted house, like a castle guarding its corner, seemed for example to have a history and, I dreamed, a military purpose. My mistakes were many. The MRI clinic presented circular windows that probably must themselves *be* the MRIs, the torture tubes. The roof of the Sun Salon slanted down not with tinted skylights but with solar panels. And the Tudor Cottages Shopping Center, fronted with half-timber façades, dated back to the time of England, somehow.

Today I didn't know much better. I wished I had an adult relationship to the city. I wished indeed that I was omniscient. Some buildings I *had* been in—from the road I could glance in a neighborhood lending library and remember how the mold smelled. Other sites triggered more situational memories—the cascading all-important Woodward Park where I and my several friends had warrens of rosebushes to run through. But I had never been rich in adventures. I grew up on the backyard system. I had been shuttled in cars.

I remembered when I went to the doctor as a little kid—my pediatrician was up on the eleventh floor of the same medical complex we were headed to now—I gazed down, standing for five minutes at a time trying to orient myself at the doctor's big picture window. I could see the river and a few familiar office towers and a seabed of trees, but no houses: the houses were there of course, beneath the trees, but I didn't know that. I did recognize the fancy shopping center immediately below us, with its English telephone booths like little red knobs—but then behind the shopping center there was an open field, and behind that field there was a second, and with a shock I wondered if anyone had ever gone to that field before, or if it was known to man, or was on any maps. Of course it was Cascia Hall's soccer field, a perfectly well-known place.

And I never knew what direction my house was in. In a city of cars, when you don't know how to drive, when you've been driven everywhere, seat-belted, orientation is rare. It's a deep, slanting science, a source of anxiety, a thing that you fumble for but can't bring yourself to grasp.

Kim and I were in the elevator going up—it was exactly like a dream, a high school reunion transposed to my childhood doctor's office. It was no longer pediatrics, of course, the hospital had shuffled its departments—but it was the same physical space, the same layout, the same windows. Kim took a call from some guy named Randall, and I stood at what seemed like the same old window: There was the shopping center with its little red telephone booths. Looking out, I saw the Arkansas River clock through the Thirty-first, the Forty-first, and then the Sixty-first Street bridges, after which the river bent away, so that only with my cheek pressed to the window frame could I follow it all the way out to the 101st Street bridge. I stepped back and contemplated the scattered office buildings rising from the trees. I tried to remember their names, and the intersections. It pleased me to line up the landmarks on the unseen grid of streets that was spread out, like a net, beneath the blowing tops of the trees.

Kim covered her receiver with a smile. "You go on in first. He'll be so excited to see you."

Jamie was in a windowless room, watching TV. The TV was bolted to the ceiling, and Jamie sat up in bed looking at it, his remote poised. He glanced at me and then back to the TV, and almost changed the channel, but didn't. He looked to see what exactly I wanted.

And he recognized me.

I should have had some line. But it was all I could do to stand there and be looked at.

Flustered to present himself, Jamie lifted his far buttock off the mattress and reached for my hand. "What's up." His eyes were candid, except that he kept glancing down at his lap, looking for something.

"Guess who brought me here. Kim Wheel." That was the first thing I said. As if the smaller irony were enough to account for the larger.

We tried to catch up. I spotted his wedding ring— which Kim had told me to look for. Jamie and his wife wanted to move to New York, or maybe New Jersey: "Melissa and I are going to try to get teaching jobs there," he told me.

I sighed. "And me"—I raised my eyebrows—"I'm thinking maybe I should move back here."

Jamie welcomed that. He could be perfectly pro-Tulsa. He told me how downtown was about to undergo a big revitalization. There were lofts, he said, and apartments, "just like a big city." He smiled. "You move home, and I'll move to New York. Reverse brain drain."

Jamie had met his wife at a comic book convention. She studied nursing at OSU Tulsa, but then went back and became a kindergarten teacher. He was still finishing his computer science degree: he would use it to teach high school. I remarked that my parents, who as Jamie knew were also teachers, had retired and moved away to sunny Galveston. "It's as if Tulsa never happened, for them," I said.

Jamie made a dry spitting sound.

I further bewailed my parents. "It's, like, didn't they make any friends here?"

"Their friends probably all moved to Phoenix."

Jamie and I were bonding. "I got to go to a study-abroad thing in Germany," I told him, "and in Germany they stick to even their elementary school friends—forever. You'll be at a bar and then your friend gets an SMS and he's like, 'That's Georg, from the village. Georg's going to join us.'"

Jamie nodded his head sagely.

I went on: "But in America it's like we're always supposed to disappear—if we reach, you know, a certain level of success. Like Elijah. It's like, if we're valedictorian we have to get assassinated—because effectively we get up and give a speech and then we disappear to some faraway university. All our major social institutions growing up are about building intense friendships over a limited period of time and then severing them. High school, and then college. And summer camp. Poof. My parents, having completed their careers successfully, move."

I was in a way bragging. But Jamie said that he too had lost touch with tons of people—and he had not gone anywhere. Occasionally he would run into someone at the store. At video rental stores, especially. One of our very smartest classmates had recently gotten a job as a reporter for the local news. "I see her on TV sometimes."

"Of course," I said, "we talk about losing touch with people but we didn't even know them at the time, probably."

"Except for her." He gestured at Kim, who was standing in the door. "And she still knows everybody."

We turned and watched Kim pull up a chair. It was as if we were two old gumshoes and Kim was the attractive lady who had come in to consult with us. She seated herself neatly. Kim Wheel had always been much more popular than Jamie Livingstone or Jim Praley. And having her there changed the dynamic. She was catching up with Jamie on his condition. His treatment was nearing its end, apparently. But I wasn't really listening.

"Do you remember Adrienne Booker?" I abruptly asked Jamie.

"No."

Kim looked up. "You remember her, Jamie. She went to Franklin."

"She did?"

"She kept a low profile," I said, "but she was friends with like Chase Fitzpatrick."

He opened his mouth as if in epiphany, but it didn't come. He closed his mouth again.

"She dropped out early, but you might remember her, she did all this art stuff," I said. "Oil family. She used to eat lunch by herself—by the prefabs?"

"Oh!—she was in that one play." He jammed his fingers into the mattress trying to remember the name of the play. I wished he would give me a hint. But my eyes wandered behind his bed, to where someone had pinned up a wall of photos. I wanted to get a look at Jamie's wife. The photos appeared recent, and a preponderance featured a party of some kind, held outdoors under a bright blue tarp. A small shoal of people: I hesitated to say which one would have married my old bus-stop friend. I couldn't tell. None of the revelers in the photographs seemed to be aware that they were in a movie about social entropy, and missed connections, and loneliness. Helga—as I dubbed the heavily bespectacled, fist-pumping one, the one who seemed to be caught in some exhortative pose in every picture, and whom I figured not for the wife but for some kind of auntie ringleader—she presented herself not as the ringleader of a marginalized or embittered minority, but of a happy, normal, self-sufficient group of friends.

Jamie snapped his fingers. "She tore apart her children! A tallish blond girl."

"*Medea*? Wow." How excellent Jamie was to recall this. "I have zero memory of that. But that's definitely her though—like a Greek tragedy or something."

We told Jamie what had happened to Adrienne.

"I actually flew here to see her," I put in.

"So you guys . . . ?"

I nodded, as if thrown into reverie. "Summer after freshman year of college."

Jamie waited.

"I met her at a party," I allowed. I expected the impact of my feeling to speak for itself. Saying it out loud seemed like curtailing the force of it. "We dated that summer," was all I said. I wanted the room to swirl around us, to pop up with life-sized dioramas depicting the Blumont, the couch at the studio, the Booker terrace. Perhaps I paused for a second too long. Jamie contracted, and perceived something in my eyes: I had looked forward far too long to this. Quite specifically: to impressing him.

"Okay," he said. "And you've kept in touch . . ."

"Actually, no."

Jamie almost laughed. It was weird. He repressed it. He smiled, his small face blushed.

I had put myself in a weak position, and it seemed to stress him out and he blinked, tossing his hair out of his eyes.

Kim didn't realize what had happened. She was outlining some of the difficult questions surrounding Adrienne's rehab. Jamie was bored.

"Your friend's related to the Booker Petroleum family, right? So, I mean—no point getting mixed up in that."

Kim seemed surprised. "With Lydie Booker, you mean?"

Jamie spoke out in the loud bored singsong that people use to intone obvious wisdom: "If Lydia Booker gives you a *dime,* she will start running your business." He explained, "My sister-in-law works for the Greenwood Foundation. Lydia Booker gave them ten thousand dollars. Six months later they almost wanted to give it back. They actually had a meeting to discuss that option. And this is other nonprofits too. She has a reputation."

"What was the problem?" I quickly asked.

"I don't know. She had her own guy she wanted to be the speaker at this big gala thing. She had this great idea, she didn't see what the problem was."

"Tulsa's evil grandmother," I joked, my voice trembling.

"Exactly."

I made an exaggerated gesture, drawing a pretend

cigarette to my lips, and blinked my eyes in Lydie's exhausted, imperious way.

Jamie didn't get these physical references. But Kim smiled. "I do think Lydie can be like that." She was nodding. "That's part of why Adrienne isn't that close to her—Adrienne totally doesn't have this like controlling . . ."

"Power thing?"

Kim's eyes lit up. "Yes."

"Really?" My voice squeaked. I went on, in a quieter voice. "But the things about Lydie that strike you as domineering are the same things about Adrienne that I love. I mean, when I met her I realized—to be an artist, you can imagine—you have to understand—she has this kind of regal thing."

"Maybe you should marry into the family," said Jamie.

I must have blushed.

"I just mean—"

"No, no worries. It's true. It was aspirational when I first dated her. Adrienne lived in a skyscraper. And that she didn't go to college—to never go in the first place, you know, in our day and age. It blew my mind."

"Because it's stupid," said Jamie.

"Well. You're preparing for life as a public school teacher, Jamie. You have a certain outlook."

"I'm just saying you have to be pretty fucking loaded to consider not going to college. Has she ever supported herself?"

I was speechless.

"You would like her, Jamie," said Kim. Kim was so smart.

"I'm just saying not everyone can afford to just blow off college, that lifestyle."

A long silence ensued. It was humid. A monkey chittered, coming from another room's TV.

"Adrienne screened a video one time," I began. My voice was tight and flat. "She's on a sidewalk at night, right north of here. In that section between Cherry Street and 244." I looked at him. "She was naked."

I crossed my legs.

"The camera zooms in on her face, and then zooms out on her body, back and forth. Her face is serious, like she knows that she's naked. You understand there is nothing erotic about this. In fact it was hard to watch— she was screening it just for me. It goes on for five minutes. At the end, the cameraman kneels down, and you get like a monumental shot from below, her standing there looking off into the distance, and that's it."

"You made that movie?"

"No, no, Chase did. Chase Fitzpatrick."

"They never got caught?"

"No, of course not. We didn't do it to get caught."

Kim was politely holding her breath. I could tell from Jamie's face that he thought this was all the stupidest and perhaps most obnoxious thing he had ever heard of.

"You see," I said, "she made *me* do a movie like that. Once."

Jamie frowned. "Was this like an initiation rite?"

"No. It was art. I mean. It was midnight before we

191

were going to go, and I was like, 'Aren't we going to have some drinks?' 'No,' Adrienne said, 'you have to be mindful.' She said I had a performance to give. And Chase—who was sort of the other man, you understand—was coming over with the night filter. Soon I was in the passenger seat and I was like, I guess I have to take my clothes off. They had a good spot—the street was dark, all the houses were built up on these really steep front yards, with steps down to the sidewalk. So I wasn't walking past anyone's picture window.

"And it was my show. To direct. So I made Chase get out and train his camera on the passenger-side door. I meant to count to a hundred but could only make it to ten, and then I stepped out, as confident as if I was in a business suit. And I tried to keep up that briskness. I think it was really comedic, for a while—which is not what I wanted. I had to go up to the corner, cross, and come back down. I had Chase shooting me, you know, and here I was." I gestured.

"It's one of those things, like you realize . . ." I stared away, the talk dead in my mouth. I took a deep breath.

They were silent. Kim looked odd, leaning way over on her elbow. She didn't know what to say.

"Maybe too much information," I said.

"No no." Jamie tried to chuckle.

Street Fighter, as we called this series, did not exist on the internet. I had one copy, on an old VHS tape. Other than that, Adrienne might have a copy. I hoped she did.

At least I could say I had opened up to them.

Jamie had said little about his prognosis, but from what Kim said, it was decent. He would lead a normal life. He would just need someone who could always come take care of him, for a night or two at a time. And judging by those photos on his wall, he would have someone. It looked quite possible that Jamie Livingstone from the bus stop would in middle age be better provided-for in love and companionship than Adrienne Booker.

I was flying back to New York the next morning. It didn't seem real. For the first time since I landed in Tulsa, the sky was overcast, and seemed to wad like a layer of protective cotton over all our little buildings and roads. Kim had driven down to the river, to the efficiency apartment where she told me she lived. I was headed downtown. But on the way I stopped at the time-honored record store, Starship Records & Tapes.

Starship had once been a house, small and peak-roofed, and retained its creaking wooden floors, its chopped-up floor plan. Most of the CDs were locked in glass cases, built in along the walls. I had to ask for help, and the clerk, not having heard of Adrienne, suggested I try the clearance bins. There it was. *Patience,* the album was called, by Adrienne Booker. It was loose in a cardboard box labeled LOCAL ARTISTS.

I got back into my car and slid Adrienne's CD into the stereo. I didn't want to play the stereo very loud. My windows were down. I didn't want to blast anything. In fact I wasn't positive that the music even was Adrienne's. I checked the jewel case. Her live performances had been so brash, so off-putting, whereas what I was hearing now was normal, a tangy drum-and-guitar thing.

Live shows had always been the point. The word was paint to her, and as a vocalist she pushed and smeared and lashed it, pronouncing and repronouncing a lyric, ironizing it and jinxing it, or singing it like liturgy, solemn and black. Or she was violent—hacking out the rhythm. She never believed in expressing feelings, I knew: the thing that captured the crowd was her cold manner. If she moved a muscle it was controlled, never blurred. Even when, from her ululations, I expected her to be freaking out—I would look at the stage and see a stately figure, glancing at her audience. She always stood still while she sang, as if posing for a portrait—like *Mona Lisa,* or like Washington on the dollar bill.

I was passing under the inner dispersal loop when something made me turn the stereo back up. This was I believe the second song, and much softer than the previous: the voice that tacked above the drums sounded like Adrienne's own. Not sawing as it used to do, but sailing.

For the first time since I arrived in Tulsa, I was hearing her. I pulled over to the curb and stopped—the street was so dead. "It's too soon for morning," Adrienne sang. Here was the ideal mythic instance of the singer-songwriter: that she is in trouble and has put her voice down to be found, by an ex-boyfriend perhaps, when he comes back looking for her. But it was not like Adrienne was speaking to me, not at all: She had never spoken like this. This was as if I peeked in her diary and discovered that she secretly formed her sentences with great care—speaking to us meanwhile in jottings and interjections and acting distracted. She had never had the mind of a diary-keeper. She had never talked like this: "I am trying, I am trying / To make it work / Because you love me." Her voice was different physically too, it was shallower than it used to be, and that did more to bring me up short than anything. It was as if she had tied something inside her and fastened up the collar of her throat.

My phone rang. It was Lydie. "Jim," she said, "can I consult with you about a couple of things?" She was saying something about Rod, I tried to understand what. My reception was horrible, so I turned the stereo off and climbed out of my car, hurrying down the sidewalk in hopes of finding a better signal. I had the skyscrapers before me. "Hello," I kept saying, "Lydie?" Lydie was about to go into a meeting, but wanted to know if I was available to stay with Adrienne again. There was some problem with Rod—we would have to discuss it all, she said, after her meeting—this meeting with Texas—which was going to last all afternoon.

"Shall I just drop by your office later?"

She was surprised.

"I'm nearby," I said.

"Well come by if you want. We should be done about six."

Now that I was on my feet, I kept walking. I wished I had earphones and could listen to Adrienne while I walked our old routes. For here I was. "I am trying, I am trying / To make it work," I sang in an undertone on the empty street. A quarter-hourly carillon of church bells bloomed out, and wafted down as it could, between the buildings.

The Performing Arts sign was still exploding: *La Bohème* was here again, boom boom boom. A friend of mine who had lived all over once defined the true city as a place where you can sing on the street and not seem crazy. But there wasn't even anyone on the Tulsa street, to hear you sing. Simply to be on foot was enough to look like a crazy person. I heard a car turn the corner behind me. I remembered when I had been to no city but this one. At that age—you wouldn't mind to *seem* crazy.

Which is what Adrienne had done so resolutely, in effect, with so much courage and poise. From her friends at the hospital I got no impression of her edge, of the instant sharpness of her spontaneity. She cut my hair once, while I was napping. She demonstrated—what? Presence, ultimately, leaps of faith landing with her silent sense of moment. The way she used to walk down the street. I wondered if I saw her now—if I was one of the Texans up there meeting with Lydie, and I came down to the street for a smoke break and saw Adrienne walking by, a young woman of arch deportment, the perfectly sedate expression on her face, the bags under her eyes, the heels and skirt.

A businessman might feel flirted with. Adrienne's image might stick in his mind. But later probably, in remembering—a businessman might think he saw through Adrienne, with her flamboyant skirts and her stiff neck.

I remember once in the studio when Adrienne was

painting she turned to me. "Do you really think I'm good?"

She had her paintbrush in her hand and wet paint on it when she asked me.

Maybe she had been wasting her life. I stepped onto Main, and a long-held breath began to flow: all the lights turned green, and the cars ahead of me as well as other clumps down the line came loose and began to roll. And then were gone. The road itself, being one-way, was free of yellow lines, and stretched across calmly, curb to curb, with the dignified tautness of a preacher's back.

I marched on.

This street used to be dirt, the ground for roughnecks who on payday tottered down the road spilling their buckets of beer, shying up to storefronts, peering into the new-built porticos of banks and two-story office buildings. There used to be a trolley line. It all got cleaned up, though. The last spontaneous thing that happened here was a race riot. Before our parents were born. Now it's so clean that even our town boosters have decided it's boring, and will talk about that, and vote ballot initiatives back and forth to tear up pavement and plant a pedestrian mall or to repave it and put traffic lights back in a decade later.

I wish there could be more to it. I can eke some poetry out, but when the world ends people are going to remember this part of Tulsa as a dry run. I had used downtown as the backdrop to a love story—but most people aren't so willful. At their roots, the skyscrapers are dumb. What a relief it had once been to slide my arms beneath Adrienne's back, to spread apart her shoulder blades.

I neared the Center of the Universe and began to climb uphill toward the skater's plaza. Rod used to send Adrienne to Massachusetts for ballet camp, she told me. But when Rod himself moved house to New England, she stopped. That was her pride. She was so graceful, compared to Rod: she might have gone to ballet camp forever. I imagined she had the body for it. After Rod left, she took to roaming the streets at night. She could have become something horrible. But she didn't. That was her pride. There were special limitations in her character, internal walls that she respected. On those walks that governed Adrienne's mornings, we sometimes stopped at the Center of the Universe to watch the skaters. They would already be at work—they were skipping school, was why they had to get there so early; they had to make a show of leaving home and then they had to go somewhere. I had always wanted to know skaters—I soon learned to smile at their seriousness, the way they would lean over like a hawk, arms spread, or cradle the air in front of them as they balanced; I loved the earnest way they cursed, as if their dads were watching. They knew who Adrienne was from their older brothers. And anyway they had always seen Adrienne at any good party they had ever been to. They talked to her as they might talk to a friend's very hot mother. They would coast near, and one time she even held out her hand like a queen, and let herself be kissed, just to make fun of me the way I was watching.

This afternoon the Center of the Universe was empty except for its clanking flagpole. I took a deep breath. I wanted to try, like Adrienne, to sing. I started out quietly—humming, almost. But you have to do it kind of loud for it to be "singing." Behind me I had the sky-scrapers, mute and dumb, and out before me the bricky warehouse district rippled in the heat. I started in my mouth, droning like Adrienne had taught me. I sounded like a Ouija board talking. I forced myself to form a syllable, blunting the sound into consonants. I stepped forward. It was like winding up a pitch: "New York, New York, New Yooork." The "New-Yuhhh . . ." combi-nation was easy, but then I had to lower my jaw, eye-brows raised, as the "Yuh" widened into "Yor." My real life was waiting, in New *Yoooork*. Or?

I could see what Adrienne liked about singing: I had to go to the most confident thing in my stomach, the warmest and wettest thing, in order to open up my throat. An electric impulse in the brain has to ignite in the lungs, as by analogy the antennae tips on buildings flash red—as if stinging the air with red-hot ideas, as if that was what made the waves sizzle in the air.

I walked abashed, in the glare of my half-dead epiphanies, to the rail of the plaza. I leaned against it and looked back at the skyscrapers. I was not going to sing. I did not have the same insides as Adrienne—that much was clear. But if only she had ever looked up at this view and wanted it as bad as I did. When I first heard that she crashed, I thought it might have been the most ballsy kind of suicide, throwing the bike out from be-neath her. But that was wrong—that was a confusion I had made between her high autonomous daredevilry and real heart, real autobiography. It was much more like her, precise even in the absence of stimuli, to try to follow her own road and flip, mistaken perhaps but poised, through the air like a mannequin.

At six p.m., the sun angled its neck, and the Booker's art deco carvings sliced in relief like fresh lacerations—the skin of a Mayan temple.

All of this was real to me: the brass bench in the lobby, the smooth black floor. Everyone had gone home at five. The receptionist must have wondered why I crossed the floor so slowly and ceremoniously: it was the lento of self-destruction, watching in slow-motion for the shoe-box diorama to bend, the cardboard breaking beneath the weight of my sole, canceling the remembered version of this space.

"I'm here to see Ms. Booker. She's in a meeting, but I was told I could wait."

The upstairs secretary had never heard of me.

"Tell them it's about her niece—Lydie's expecting me."

The elevator rattled upward like a self-assertive little machine. I pressed a number I had never pressed before, 18, a fat sans-serif numeral like the others, stenciled onto a yellowed translucent button that looked forever dirty, like an old bone die. I ran my hand over the whole array, up to the decorative panel above it, which was stippled with a corona of little gold indentations, dots fading up asymmetrically like the arm of an art deco Milky Way. My hand looked young, and awfully pink, on the gold. Adrienne was always automatically up for a kiss in here; she liked to wave at the security camera. But now the door opened onto an office.

All was quiet, after-hours. I could hear voices, but the hallway ahead of me was empty. Brown marble tile, white veins. Everything was ugly: radiators and other fixtures of the same vintage as those in our public schools, built during the same boom. But everything here had lasted better and was cleaner. Up ahead of me two men in suits, the voices I had heard, emerged from what must have been a men's room, and then disappeared around a corner. I dropped back and then followed them around that corner, and saw a grand padded door close behind them. And there in front of that door was the secretary.

She showed me to a couch; I immediately got up and asked for the bathroom. After I washed my face it still looked like I had been crying. It was the lack of sleep. I could draw some strength from the rooms just two stories above, the bedroom where I had spent so many authoritative nights—but I had decided not to think about that. Adrienne didn't live there anymore, they said. She lived in Los Angeles. When I came back out I sat down and was quiet. The secretary was playing solitaire.

I had been sitting in silence for an hour when finally Lydie and the others came out. They were finished. There was agreeable chuckling as the door opened and Lydie strode out smiling; her smile seemed to increase when she noticed me—but she made no sign. I couldn't tell who were her staff and who were the Texans until Lydie showed a number of them to a side door, mentioning that they would find refreshments in the refrigerator, and she referred to something that I thought was perhaps a conferencing device, and then she turned to

201

face me as the remaining men, her staff presumably, streamed on past her.

"Sorry Lydie—I didn't know what we needed to set up for tonight."

She smiled and knocked her head sideways, indicating a door I hadn't seen before. It was small, but the room beyond it was magnificent. "I have to take those men out to dinner," Lydie was saying. These windows! I had always seen them from the outside, floor-length windows wrapping around the neck of the Booker—they constituted one of the key details in the Tulsa skyline. I remember, when Adrienne first asked me up to the penthouse, I was a little disappointed that its windows weren't these. But to look out from them now was humbling: because we were level with the buildings at each of the intersection's corners, the main thing you ended up looking at was other offices.

I had been trying to reconstruct in my hour on the couch wistful things people had told me about the prewar office spaces of New York, tight bookish places with ceiling fans—spaces cast off only recently in favor of newer offices with energy-saver lights and ergonomic chairs. Booker Petroleum had chairs carved from wood, muscled like animal parts; the ceiling was high and dark. Lydie, with her crinkled black shift, would have suggested something much more austere; she really could have been a gallerist, a crow in a white box. But the way I saw her sit now, the way she gripped the arm of her armchair with a buckled air of possession, her neck upright and a washed, offhand seascape hanging behind her, it was clear she had assimilated it all and emphasized a way to be herself in Tulsa, keeping the office together the way she might have a family.

"That's by Rod."

"Hm?"

She jacked her thumb at the seascape behind her.

"Rod's a painter?"

"He was." Lydie's chair squeaked. She regarded me. I liked the idea that she was evaluating me.

"You said something about Rod on the phone."

She twisted her chair away, as if caught off guard. Her meeting had clearly gone well, and maybe she had let herself forget about the hospital. "Rod isn't going to be there tonight," she told me.

"Something's the matter?"

She looked bored. "I don't know." She had picked up a wand-sized microphone, which she mashed up into her chin. "Adrienne needs to wake up soon. But she's going to be fine. She's stable, that's the important thing." Then she spoke into the little microphone: "I'll be out in five minutes."

"Is there a problem with anesthesia?"

"No, they had her murmuring some."

She just doesn't want to wake up, I thought. "But Rod. Where's Rod going to be?"

"He wants it to be my turn."

I frowned, unimpressed with this logic.

"Jim," she said, "the point is, Rod won't be there tonight. And I need to sleep."

Once again, I was to show up at eleven.

"I want to give you some money for meals," she was saying.

"Lydie," I began. "I wanted to ask you how the meeting went—"

"Yes, while I was sitting there I had a flashback to our discussion this morning: Gilbert was speaking, and I wondered, where's our Jim?" She laughed.

"I should have come up, then. I was walking around downtown, getting reacquainted with the sights."

She smirked. "The sights?"

"Yes."

"Yes," she said, "you should have come up. You could have learned something." She drew herself up. "Now, I know you're flying back in the morning, and I don't want you to overstrain yourself."

"I'm not sure I want to go back to New York, Lydie."

She held my eyes.

"Lydie—I wanted to ask you, do you think I might be able to get a job at Booker Petroleum?"

She looked blank. "Yes?"

"I guess I wanted to at least ask. I don't mean to be impertinent—I'm just excited and—I don't know, I'm very curious to ask."

"You want a job." She was stirred.

"I think I would."

"Tell me more."

"Well." I clawed the air in front of my face—as students do, when they feel they're really grappling with a question. "I might make a life for myself in Tulsa."

She stared at me. I hoped she believed me.

"Or if you know of any other opportunities in Tulsa—"

"No, no." She waved that idea away. "But your obligations at the magazine."

"I think my boss would understand."

"Understand what?"

"That I belong out here."

Lydie waited to make sure I was finished, and then she raised her eyebrows, as if skeptical, almost as if she was offended. She looked out the windows for a few seconds. "Does this have anything to do with Adrienne?"

"No. Not in any direct way."

She smiled. "The meeting met our expectations," she said. She had become very brittle; the warmth from the earlier part of our conversation, the afterglow from her meeting, had faded. "We'll be dropping heat wells in the ground all over northeast Oklahoma. And I'll lay people off to facilitate the merger."

"Okay. I understand."

She smiled at her lap, her gray hair tousling down. "But I think I could take on another assistant, in the process. I don't know if it's quite the sort of work you're expecting."

"I'd love to hear what you have."

"Jim, you seem like a very ambitious person."

"Yes."

She was cautious, gently nodding. She spread her hands apart. "I don't know what advice to give you. This is something you just came up with?"

"I've always wanted to come back." I waved at the air. "My life in New York is completely frivolous."

She nodded, bobbling her head sideways and at different angles, considering.

"Okay. So let's talk in the morning."

It was time to stand, but I didn't know if I could face the drop behind me. I got up though, and saw that dusk was falling. The windows had turned reflective. The scene was done, we were silent now, she in her shift and me in my nice pants, reflected, each moving with the poise that actors take on in theater, the office like a set, me stepping out of her way: she comes around the desk and I follow, and I'm the one to pull the door behind us.

Driving back to the hospital, I was head to toe the modern applicant, my skinny arm on the gearshift, my spherical head too improbable for anything but the cartoon of contemporary life. I treated myself to more of the rooftop whiskey at St. Ursula's, not to celebrate my success with Lydie so much as to celebrate my careering life. It always went most out of control exactly when it landed. I went down only when the whiskey had sufficiently blurred my grandiosity, such that I felt nineteen and twenty-four in the same breath.

Adrienne lay twinkling in the lights of her monitors. I stared. And then I went out onto the ward to get coffee.

"Well here you are," I said, coming back. "Would you like some coffee?" I had brought two cups.

Adrienne had been asleep for days. And on so much medication, she would dream. In her dream she would hear us, and in her sleep would misconstrue. Her head would sag, heavy with medication, encrusted and scared, smeared with confusion. She hadn't spoken coherently since her injury, Lydie said. Nor supposedly had she been cognizant to understand anything. Yet she was fighting, according to the rhetoric. She churned. I thought she probably guessed.

She had murmured, when they fitted her with her neck brace, "No water, no water, no water"; Lydie and Rod had both mentioned this to me. It was a rumor started by the doctors, and it was supposed to be proof of her orneriness surviving.

I dragged a plastic armchair over to the bedside, pushed it completely flush with the rail, and added a pillow so I could sit level with the bed.

"You may wonder why I've come here," I said. I noticed a MasterCard-sized sensor that had pulled partway loose above her breast, and I leaned forward to fix it. The irritation there was crosshatched and red. But I pressed the sensor back down.

While craned over, I wanted to pull up her blanket for her. I held my breath. There were so many bandages, and they rustled as I pulled. I dragged her blanket up to her neck, and then I plopped back into my chair.

"You wonder why I've come here." I took up the second cup of coffee and held it in my steepled hands; I forced myself to drink. Then, a toast. "To Adrienne Trismegistus Thrice-Greatest. Killer of Indians. Dinosaur and friend. Old triceratops."

I had hitched up my pants and went out to the bathroom once more. The urinal was sculpted and clean. Once upon a time, I remembered, I tried to write Adrienne the most beautiful emails. They may not have made much sense to her, but a Saturday afternoon would go, composing one. It was the joy of that semester back at college. I was never so fluent. Or so accomplished, as after staying up all night, when I wandered the campus at dawn feeling spent, as if I had just written a term paper or something. I wandered the public parks going over what I had written in my head. Out of all of it there was only one line I could still remember: "The connections between us, Adrienne, are more intricate and more awesome than I am, on my own." She never let me write drivel like that when we were dating.

She had been a better editor than college—Adrienne stood up and intimidated me more than college ever dared to. She wanted to be the opposite of a meritocracy: born wealthy, mostly unfriendly, but agog with unearned talents. After I met her I tried to go ahead and be like her, running ahead of myself like a dog, barking, looking back at its dull human master and wondering why he couldn't keep up. I could write a new college application essay:

When my ex-girlfriend broke her back in a motorcycle accident, I learned many things about myself. I learned how to relax. I learned that my girlfriend had probably completely forgotten about me. And I remembered how honorable she was, and true. I realized I had never taken it upon myself to sit and watch her sleep. I had never stood still. I had never let myself doubt her; I had never stood still and stared at her before. I should have.

I wondered how many more days Adrienne might sleep. I wanted very badly to talk to her. And yet I could leave tomorrow and she might never know I had been here. Lydie might think less of me if I disappeared, but that wouldn't matter.

A nurse was in Adrienne's room. She jumped when I entered.

"Hey," I said. This nurse was checking and re-plugging some of Adrienne's wires—like a switchboard operator would, in a hurry. She left the blanket folded back, as it had been before I ever got here.

The room smelled like Windex now. With the night nurse gone the room fell deathly quiet, except I could hear some heat pipes. Or rather it was something in this room, perhaps some new medical equipment, clicking and knocking—I looked—or I thought it might be Adri-enne's pants, the astronaut pants that kept her blood flowing, pockets filling and refilling with air—but the astronaut pants were not going, actually. They had been turned off.

I got up and walked around to the other side of the bed. Adrienne's left forearm—the one wrapped in its cast, braced up to the fingertips in a steel splint—wobbled from the elbow. Her arm was having a kind of slow spasm or something; it was knocking against the alu-minum part of the bedrail at slow, clip-cloppy intervals.

"That's very spooky of you," I murmured, grasping her bedrail. I wondered if I envied her, lying there. "Soon you'll be transformed," I told her. "It won't take long. The old Adrienne will cease to exist. You'll grow new skin, new bones. So and so. They may even fit you with retractable claws."

"What about my hands?"

It was her. It was a pencil flung off the penthouse rail and I had to fly—

"—Your hands are beautiful."

She rang the casted hand so violently against its rail that I jumped backwards.

"Not this," she said, flailing it against the rail.

"Your cast," I hissed, seizing it, trying to keep her from breaking it, "it's in a cast."

"I can't see," she explained, almost conversationally. Time raced outside, and I stared at her open mouth, alive now with its characteristic contours, grimacing. Hoarse, heaving: She didn't know what to do. She didn't know who I was.

"Should I get a nurse?"

Her blindfolded face managed to wither, as if impatient.

"It hurts," she said.

"I know." I was still gripping her left hand.

She drew up her lip. Her gums were marvelous, like the reddest part of a watermelon. "You're in the way," she panted, "you're all in my way." She was beginning now to try to scoot up on her other elbow, as if to rise, and then she gave that up, and began instead to gesture with her free right hand pointing upward and left, and then coming down clumsy, finlike, on her mask; I groped vaguely to catch it and seized that hand too, pulling it away.

"Adrienne."

She strained to shake her hand out of my grip, but I wouldn't let go. I could feel all the separate flexors roiling beneath my fingers like a piano, a silent appassionato. This was finally Adrienne. Her lips were twisting, twisting and relenting. "Go get a nurse," she finally gasped. I obeyed; I let go of her arms and was almost out the door when I stopped and turned back—she thought I was gone. Craftily, she crooked her bare arm out from the sheets and suddenly tore at the mask. The blue mask snapped askew, quite crooked on its strap. She struck it again, agile now with her thumb about to hook beneath it—I was back at the bed and yanked that hand backwards, her cast arm rose, and I had to wrestle my elbow down for leverage, holding both her arms now, my torso beached halfway on top of hers, restraining her completely. My face hovered above her face: her bruised cheekbone stood out where the mask had been, the skin there looked raw, I would have to replace the eye mask exactly in its old outline—and coming out under the edge of the eye mask was her eye—what should have been the white of her eye but was red, a lake of red, and the blinking lid was black.

"It's for medical purposes," I breathed, trying to sound authoritative. "Don't hurt your—fuck!" She stabbed her free thumb into my arm and gouged upward, at the blood vessels below my wrist. I let go for a second and then I shook her unhurt arm so hard I feared I would break it.

"Adrienne!"

The eye mask's elastic band had slipped over the widest point of her head and was now beginning to contract, slowly inching itself off. While I lay there, the

212

section of eye that I could see increased, and within the red came a razor-thin wisp of blue, the gassy corona about a dead black star, the dilated pupil, a hole in space. Falling, my face had to fix itself. I did and didn't want her to recognize me. For all I knew her vision was deranged. Quick as I could I released the hand that was in the cast and reached to replace her mask. The eye, blinking weakly, snapped itself together. The iris contracted, and took on a look of intelligence. In the instant that I replaced the mask, I wondered if she had seen me.

Her free cast flew back and came down on the side of my head, and her legs began to shake as if uncontrollably. I should have called a nurse but it hurt too much, even to laugh at the blow, and so I plunged my head into the pillow beside her ear. "Adrienne. Is this the first time you've been awake?" She was silent. Her ear was silent. My head was smarting. "Listen," I said, in a voice that seemed flooded to me with my own identity. I had stopped whispering. "Do you know what's happened?"

Her lips stiffened.

"You know you are in the hospital?"

"Yes." Her breath was like a foul warm wind. "I thought I was blind."

"You broke your back."

She spasmed again, a mechanical insistence of life, and then raised her casted hand high to strike the bedrail, making a mighty knell that filled the ward. I let it fall and then I closed in on her, my chest across her chest, my arms across her arms, my head beside her head, until, like a propeller winding down, her body shuddered and her spasm stopped. My head was almost kissing her. I

213

pulled back slightly, and saw her lips puckered, as if on the point of an idea.

Then a strong orange arm pulled me away, and the nurse tabbed the spigot that controlled Adrienne's morphine, letting two slugs drain into Adrienne's blood. "You should have called me," the nurse said, as Adrienne's eyes, underneath the mask, probably closed.

"She was awake."

The nurse surveyed Adrienne. "Well. You calmed her down."

"Did I hurt her?"

The nurse stiffened. She was an older woman, she was strong, her tanned skin creased at her elbow and wrists.

"She was trying to take her mask off, so I had to restrain her."

"You've been drinking."

"Is it on my breath? It stays on your breath."

The nurse stood there, considering.

"Did she hit you? You're bleeding." She examined my head. I winced. The nurse came back with gauze and rubbing alcohol. "I called her mother," she said.

"Her aunt? Lydie said she was going to try to sleep—"

"Well, she's on her way."

"I wish you had asked. I mean, is this an emergency?"

"She asked to be called in the event that the patient woke up."

I scraped my fingernails down my tongue, trying to get rid of the taste of whiskey. I sat down to wait. From the ding of the elevator, from her boots on the waiting room carpet, I could hear Lydie coming. She stood, draped in an unseasonable fur, filling the doorway, her face haggard and un-made-up.

"Hey Lydie."

"Is she awake?"

I explained about the morphine. Preemptively, I sketched out the scene with the eye mask and the spasm. I didn't mention that I had been drinking. Lydie shed her fur and laid it, like a blanket, across Adrienne's midsection. She listened respectfully, nodding but not giving anything away. Then she carried herself out of the room, presumably to see the nurses.

When she came back, Lydie stood for a while at the foot of Adrienne's bed. I expected her to take a chair, but she stayed intent, her arms braced on the bedrails. I wouldn't have thought Lydie needed such moments.

"What do the nurses say?" I asked.

"She'll be out for a few hours." Lydie sat down opposite me, businesslike. I saw what it was that her face was missing: the eyeliner. "Jim," she said, "we have some spare time here."

"I know you were looking forward to a good sleep," I said.

She made a very small smile and shook her head, casting her eyes back toward Adrienne. Then back to me. "So, Jim. Are you going to make your flight in the morning?"

"I don't think so."

"Well, I think it would be disingenuous to pretend that we couldn't make room for you. I still haven't talked to HR. But at the very least I could hire you out of my personal budget."

"That would be an honor."

She shifted, puissant.

"However, Jim, I want us to be candid. I don't want you to put yourself in a position where you would be frustrated. As it happens, you don't have much relevant experience or training. Nor do we have any really exciting openings at the moment."

"An exciting opening probably wouldn't be appropriate . . ."

She frowned. "Well, you could be my personal assistant."

"I would jump at that."

"It's not a glamorous job, Jim."

She waited for me to ask questions.

"What would I be doing?"

"I have different assistants and they do different things. On a task basis. So it varies. I would never ask you to organize my medicine cabinet or anything like that—I'm not talking about that sort of thing. But you might have to organize a reception, caterers and flowers. I might give you a research project and you would spend a week down in our library."

It was this easy. Lydie gave me a sense of the numbers, reminding me that the cost of living in Tulsa was much lower than that of New York. She obviously didn't know how little I had been making.

"Lydie, I have your offer."

"Well, you should think it over."

"I may have to move very fast. I probably will make up my mind tonight, and let New York know."

Lydie ordered me to get a hotel, get some sleep.

I had only $147 left in my checking account, but didn't mention this. I would use my credit card. I rose and walked out, with nothing but my wallet and rental keys in my pockets. It didn't even occur to me to go find my luggage.

The highway was empty under the stars. I drove slowly, to keep my rpm's low. My car was a fly in the great empty barn of the sky. It's a flying pig, I said. Trapped and harnessed.

Adrienne would be astonished. Nothing I could have told her—about New York, or my editing job, or my poems—would have impressed her. That had all been just a matter of showing up—indeed it was no more than what you expected, if you went to college and talked the talk. But that I asked Lydie for a job—that was a wild action, and it would run on into the future, and Adrienne would recognize in it that wild, sad thing in my nature for which she had loved me, or had been supposed to love me, that thing I had tried to convince her of. I could take satisfaction in having brought at least this part of my self up short, to rapid maturity. I realized I had made this statement. Adrienne would have to believe it.

It was good to sneak off from the hospital, to celebrate in private. I looked out off 169. That was how I selected my hotel. The Embassy Suites commanded an apron of grass between 244 and the Broken Arrow, a kind of no-man's-land unseen from surface roads. I simply drifted down the proper exit ramp and parked.

The hotel's reception desk was empty, so I strolled out under the big atrium. It yawned all the way to the top, up to a high glass skylight, an atrium banded with terraces, each floor's recessed exit sign bleary and green. It was like the inside of a space station: I remembered it, I realized. I had been here before when I was little.

Had I apparently been everywhere before—did I overdo it? Beside me there was a pool, and a tropical waterfall built on brown Oklahoma rocks. I undressed in the lobby bathroom and slipped into the water wearing just my boxers. My wallet would be handy poolside. I could wave my credit card at the receptionist whenever he or she appeared.

Underwater I could feel my hair lift up off my scalp and wave. I bounced, at the bottom of the pool, and made my way to where I could just barely stand, with my toes curled at the cliff of the deep end. I let the water lap my chin. It smelled like carpet. I was waiting to see if anyone would come out on the terraces, on the floors above. There'd be a signal, a muffled door sound, and the rattle of an ice bucket. Even though it was Adrienne I wanted to wait for. The water in the pool seemed to be tight, or actually tense. I needed her. I had touched her. If only I would let go and float, something that was out in the night would come padding in on these carpets and hit me. All the water was like a fat suit, a gelatinous square that constrained and controlled me and I wished, if that were the case, that Adrienne would come in and hit me again, splashing, beaning me with her heavy plaster cast again, and again. In case she never gets through to me again. That was what the emptiness built above me seemed to betoken. This is powerlessness, I thought, these still waters.

When I woke up it was like the ceiling had been freshly painted. As if in the blink of an eye it had turned to yogurt, and in that instant I had woken up. I was blinking. There was a rising humor. Maybe it was the unexpected luxury of the hotel bed, but I was delighted with this new job. I guessed I had done well on this trip home. I would go to work. Adrienne would recover. Maybe she would even be around some—the future spread out stunningly blank, but it was mine and I had spread it out by myself, and I felt happy about that. Wearing only a towel and my shirt from the day before, I ventured out into the lobby to try to get shaving cream and some other things. I well knew how rare it was to wake up so happy. I looked kindly at the children who were playing in the pool this morning, who were screaming and splashing in the hollowness of the hotel.

My flight to New York left at ten. If I walked straight out the lobby's sliding glass doors, wearing my towel, and hired a cab, I could make it. I cracked a private smile. I felt that way: ruinous, marooned. It was a relief, like deserting a war. The front desk attendant gave me some shaving cream and a razor. Last night I had talked to the night manager. He found me swimming, and we had a nice chat. I'm actually from here, I told him. I'm looking to come back, I'm interviewing with Lydie Booker. He was impressed. He asked me what I was looking at for housing. His sister was a real estate agent. What I'd really like, I told him, was to live in a house I'd never seen before, on a street I'd never visited.

In front of the mirror, scraping the cream from my chin, I made a serious face. I could have been a business traveler. But where is the beginning of something embarrassing? In my room there was a second bed, a bevy of towels, a piece of soap the size of a poker chip, wrapped in peach-colored foil. I surveyed my situation. Under the shower, being a good dog, I had considered a return to New York: I could always find another ticket. I thought of Adrienne. Perhaps she was up by now, sitting up in her hospital bed. I couldn't help but think about her with her skin remade, unbruised, uncut, sitting up bright and comfortable in her hospital bed. I might not know what to do with my sudden reappearance on the scene, but she would know. She would be able to receive me with the poise of a sitting queen. Coming out in a towel, I laid my phone next to a clean pad of hotel stationery. I would have to call New York now and quit.

I should probably call Marcus, as well.

He would need a new roommate, for one thing—in fact, if I got somebody in time, I could probably get out of October rent. I could send out an email—and include everybody I knew, anybody who might be arriving in New York—announcing, in fact, that I was leaving. But I did dread telling Marcus the specifics. He had listened to me talk about Adrienne enough, and could prelabel the situation: There goes Jim. Running away from life. Smart Jim, leaping to the aid of those who do not need him. Turning his back on New York. Too good for New

York. Pretending that he has some kind of ancestral homeland in the city blocks and front yards of Tulsa. Jim the Boy Scout, foisting himself on a tragically lamed ex. Basing his identity on people who do not know him. Good Jim, trying to do CPR on a dummy. I guess that's Jim's comfort zone. He makes up an imaginary girl-friend, and abandons his friends in New York. He quits his magazine because he's afraid of writing. He wants to get a "real job."

I should wait until I had spoken with Adrienne, and then call him. As long as I could report something human she had said, Marcus would respect that. As long as there was a girl involved, I thought, you were supposed to be able to be crazy.

But to work: I needed to make that part official. Dialing my boss Helen Mack I imagined her high sunny office, a normal day at work. The midtown skyscrapers out the window.

"Hello?" At the sound of her voice I imagined a certain version of myself: Able, naïve. A young man from middle America.

"Hi Helen."

To my consternation, the focus of the conversation was Adrienne's injury. Helen seemed to have guessed pretty precisely who Adrienne was in my life—a muse. Yet Helen totally underestimated the depths. Her mind flew like a magnet toward the endpoint: Would Adrienne be able to walk, and when would we know? Even after I announced I was quitting Helen only wanted to interpret this decision as a symptom of the intensity of my reaction to Adrienne's injury—a clumsy act of valor. Much to my frustration, she even said if I changed my mind in the next couple of weeks, I could come back. And she expected me to be in touch in the meantime with updates on Adrienne's recovery. It was hard to get her off the phone.

I closed my cell and curled my hand in my lap. There I was at my hotel-room desk, my phone in my lap. The wallpaper was floral, white-on-white, with matte velveteen leaves and petals. It was like a grandmother's wallpaper. I slowly reached out with my fingertips to touch it. And then with a jerk I stood up and went back to getting dressed. Earlier, I had gotten a text from Jenny: a bunch of people were meeting for lunch at a diner near St. Ursula's. I would go to that.

I admired the hubbub of my group. We were milling inside the door while the other diners, at narrow individual tables, warily watched this flock of youth. There was no waitress to be seen—I had already greeted a few of the others, especially Jenny—when I took charge and suggested we take some empty booths that waited next to the wall. And the group did move en masse with me as I stepped toward the booths. I thought Jenny would be sitting with me. But somehow I got trapped deep inside a booth with all boys, among them Nic. Next to him was a boy I had never met before but who seemed to be paid attention to, who joked, and who kept things going by being a bit mean to everyone. "Oh, I love your creamy skin, Nic. I'm so lucky to get to sit next to Nic." The guy on my left started tearing up sugar packets. I felt embarrassed after my leadership getting us to sit down here; my voice sounded loud to me, and when the waitress came I ordered with a strange, extremely loud voice. "Pass the jelly, pass the salt," I called across the table, after the food came. No one asked me who I was.

"Adrienne woke up," Nic told me.

"Was she talking?"

"Well, she's pretty weak. She was like the pope on TV. Sticking out her hand barely and trying to nod at people. She's got to get her strength up. The doctors say her body's totally overwhelmed right now. It's going to be months. But yeah, for now all she could really say was hello or thank you."

"Did she say anything at all about her injury? Did she react?"

"I dunno, people were really trying to reassure her, mostly. She smiled some, which I guess is good."

"Last night she was freaking out."

"Oh. Were you talking to her aunt?"

"I was there last night. I was the one who woke Adrienne up. And she was flailing in her bed." I looked at the others in our booth. The joker wasn't paying attention to me, but Nic had narrowed his brows.

"Was something wrong?" he asked.

"I mean, she wasn't in a good mood!" I shrugged for the benefit of the group. "Which I think is a testament. Most people when they're in the hospital they try to act brave for the people around them. But not Adrienne. She was too pissed."

"Sure." Nic looked uncertain, though.

"She didn't seem weak at all when I talked to her. She said she was in pain, and then that she thought she was blind. She's dying to take off the eye mask."

"Oh, they took it off—"

"They did?"

"Yeah, she barely opened her eyes but you could tell she could see . . ."

Nic asked the boys on his side of the booth to let him out and then he went to the bathroom. I tucked into my breakfast, but I was pretty distracted. The conversation moiled around me, and I stared at people as they talked to each other. Nobody noticed. I had a packet of photos, from the summer I dated Adrienne. They were squarish photographs, I don't remember what camera I used, but I remember getting them developed. I remember picking them up and thinking with what envy the developer must have appreciated the images of Adrienne. For she was at her best in these shiny square photographs, she was caught in them. There was an image I liked best, her arm almost out of its socket, flung in front of her face, the forearm torqued, and the pinkie sticking forward. It's a picture of ecstasy.

A plate crashed. It was a fresh plate, newly filled with food, and you could see the food bounce while the porcelain skittered. Everyone acted like it was normal but I was shocked. I was riveted in a shocked way: I guess my eyes had already been right there when it happened to crash, and I saw it hit. I wanted to leave after that. Everything made me feel super-cheap; I left a ten, without asking if that was enough. I slid out and left.

I was driving to the hospital to finally talk to

Adrienne and I was thinking about one time we had taken a pill, and we decided to hike from downtown all the way out of the city limits. We set out to walk, and left the Brady District, passing north under the inner dispersal loop, and felt good, and went up the green side of UCAT, and saw the reservoir north of Haskell. It was dry. We cut across the reservoir and got lost in a subdivision of sinuous drives and cul-de-sacs, and it started to make us feel self-conscious. There were not many white people in that neighborhood and we were feeling hot; I was rubbing my thumb between her shoulder blades, more and more urgently. We finally came out by the dumpsters of a major grocery store, and went around and walked in the sliding glass doors. It was a big wholesale place, and I had to fill out a membership to get us in. We went and tried to pick out some water; the aisles were two stories high. There were huge pallets of individual bottles, or you could buy a gallon jug, or a refill for a water cooler. We crawled in behind the pallets and plucked out a bottle of water. We were able to lie down together in the darkness where no one could see us, we had inventory on all sides. We were very calm about this—our fearless and gentle action is what I remember most—we only left because Adrienne wanted to sing. "I want to sing," she said. So we ran out of the store hand in hand but trying not to hold hands but we couldn't resist. "Should we go over there?" I pointed to the side parking lot, where there weren't any cars. But Adrienne wanted to sing really loud, she said. We looked up a taxi in a pay phone's phone book and it took us home to the penthouse. I quickly ran from room to room and opened all the windows. And then she sang and sang. I bit her nipples. But when the pill wore off I found myself holding her down on the bed: to keep her from going out on the terrace. I was afraid she wanted to jump. She swore she didn't but I didn't believe her. She was always so deep. She was always so hard on herself when she gave way. "This has been so fucking stupid," she said. "Why do we do this?"

"We don't ever have to do it again," I said. I was weeping too, of course.

"But you like it, Jim. I can tell that you always like to go through it."

"I do love it," I said—but my arms still braced her arms. She didn't struggle, though, anymore. She was disgusted. It was not so much that the drug made us happy and then sad, but that it made us especially emotionally intelligent at first, and then stupid.

Finally, I noticed that the windows were still open, and we were getting cold. I coaxed her into the tub, and we took a warm bath.

"We have to do something in penance," she said.

We decided, though it was now ten p.m. and we were as exhausted as possible, and clean, that we would put our clothes back on, and go downstairs, and make ourselves walk the same route again, all the way to the reservoir again.

"We'll walk around the reservoir once and then come back." Adrienne said this resolutely, and was tying her shoes. "We'll do it perfectly, and make it up to ourselves." I knew that on our way we would decide to go in at an all-night diner and get pancakes instead. I didn't say that though. I knew I would have to let it unfold.

But I was wrong. We trudged the circuit of the reservoir under the open stars, and dined on boiled eggs, at home, and carefully went to bed without doing or saying anything to spoil the image.

When I parked at St. Ursula's it was about one in the afternoon, and cloudy. There was fear in my chest. Now I guess I could call my parents and invite them back to Tulsa. I'm going to live here now, I could tell them. You can come visit me whenever you want.

6

I stopped. The room was empty and her bed was gone. The bed had been taken out entirely—leaving apparatus, the racks and the pouches, all with their tubes hanging bent from use.

I turned slowly, not wanting to see. Lydie's fur coat lay flung on a chair. On the desk next to Rod's snacks, Lydie had left her clipboard, bursting with half-filled-out forms.

I looked again, knowledgeably, at the pouches and tubes disconnected. Yesterday, when they took her to prep for surgery, these things had all gone with her. The pouch with the green sticker, for example, was the one I had carried in the elevator, the day before that. They didn't ever disconnect it. Its tube hung now, like a tusk of ivory, dripping.

I heard a nurse pass, and I froze. I wasn't supposed to be here. They should've locked the door before now, they shouldn't have let me in. I was not an experienced man. I did not have the grace behind me that I could reach for, the white sheet that you want, to throw over a thing like this. For myself I was finished, and I had no idea how to behave. I had no theory of the Bookers' privacy. I had floated in here, so deep. It was the rolling together of all their black holes—

Out in the corridor I walked past Lydie and then stopped, having realized. She turned too, and against the flow of traffic her figure stood out, shoulder-slanted but quite composed. She crooked her finger and we stepped out of the way, into a carpeted alcove next to the drinking fountain.

Lydie's eyes were quaking; she drew herself up and waited for a moment, before she nodded.

"She's gone."

Tears slicked my face when she said the words. "Yes," I said. My tears came like sweat. "I was just—" I started. But my voice snapped like a twig.

Lydie bobbed her head, as if trying to keep time. She had been crying too. "Well, she had a blood clot. In her leg. It's not unusual in cases like hers. But then the clot"— Lydie motioned, jerking—"can go up to the brain."

I reached and unconsciously touched the material of her cuff. "When did—?"

"I was in the room with her—but she was quiet."

I was not gasping. In fact, I was very still. I only had the instantaneous dispensing of hot tears incriminating me, in an X across my face. "Lydie, what if I'm at fault? What if I hurt her? I may have done it."

"I've asked about that. Because I didn't want there to be any question. But the doctors say what happened all happened instantly, at about noon today. Your conscience should be more than clear." Lydie had regained her composure.

"But she was shaking. I held her arms down but her legs were shaking like crazy. I had to bend her arms to keep her from hitting her mask . . . It seems like it would have come loose then—the clot."

"No."

"But perhaps that's when it was formed?"

"She was having spasms all the time. The fault lies with the hospital. It was a nurse who deactivated her pants."

I could barely take a breath, but my tongue kept moving. "The astronaut pants, I remember. She just started talking all of a sudden. I don't know. I should have thought—"

"Jim, I truly think you've been wonderful to her."

My heart bloomed with gratitude. That Lydie registered a tremor of suspicion toward me and instantly looked into it, that was good of her, deeply, sophisticatedly responsible. Good in a boss. But I also sensed that she had given me, as quickly as possible, the sum total of what attention she could spare.

I made it to the bathroom to cry. That was crossing the hall, and turning the corner. Like I was struggling with and racing to transport a spilling barrel of water. Once in the stall I locked myself in.

When tragedy comes like this, at first it is complete. You do not have to think it over, or decide what it means. For it is far ahead of you, and the very act of acknowledging it means letting go. But then it comes around again—and it goes through you and is worse than before. I stood with my fingertips splayed on either side of the bathroom stall, eyes closed, desperate to establish in my mind who Adrienne was. I couldn't even visualize her face. There was something frenzied about this. At least I could cry, I didn't have to muster that—and then I remembered her eyes opening, and her nose flattened red on the pillow. And in the morning she was at the wardrobe, racking through her clothes with conventional girlish aplomb, and talking to me.

I closed the toilet lid and sat down in the airsickness posture, with my head between my knees. I only wished I could sack up all our old experiences and give the lot, rolled up, to Lydie and Rod. Like a paper sack filled with nails. They could give it a shake. And understand how good she was. I needed everyone to be appreciative now—it was like I immediately had to build a definitive idea, a kind of mental tomb for Adrienne.

I stole out from the hospital, taking the emergency stairs that Jenny had shown me, the same stairs we had taken to the roof. I took them down, and slipped out the east lobby. My car was way on the other side of the hospital. I had no intention of taking my car. I wanted to walk myself out under the sky. It was a horror. I fled in horror. I just traversed the parking lot, and then I hiked up the grassy slope that supported the highway and followed it north, keeping just to the outside of the corrugated rail. But this did not feel very private, I was still in view of the hospital, so I waited for a lull in the traffic and then I hurried across. There were six lanes. In the distance, oncoming cars began to honk, and I felt a flash of guilt when I hopped the opposite rail—for being so showy. I jogged downhill out of view, into a grassy trough that ran along an access road.

It felt right to breathe hard. The clouds above were heavy. For the whole of that walk I was sure it would rain, but it didn't. I had time for lots of feelings. I walked the uneven grass, obviously mowed by a riding mower every month or so. I had time for that thought. I had time for lots of thoughts, and my stepping, through the tall grass, seemed to be a blundering and a rampaging through the past. To every thought of Adrienne I could now touch the fact of her death, and when I had done that to each of my thoughts I would have scotched them, to a certain extent. And that would be done.

I wished that she hadn't seen me, when that mask slipped. In her field of vision my face had been a white glob maybe, a big finger, pressing down on her. After five years of nothing.

I made it to Forty-first Street before tedium threatened to compromise my feelings. I found a curb to sit on for five minutes, and then I started back.

In the room, Rod and Lydie were standing, facing in different directions, each on the phone. Lydie waved me back out into the corridor, and then came after me, taking my arm. She was taking a consolation call— acknowledging, lugubriously, "Yes. It's the truth. You're right Frieda." But all the while her movements were frantic. She marched me right into the elevator.

Once it closed behind us, Lydie leaned her head back

against its wall. She was newly old. Her expression reminded me of my departed grandmother's: the sad, satisfied way elderly women smile—as if at a remove. It made me feel impotent, as a grandchild—as if I was merely an ornament at the end of her life. I was sad to see it on Lydie: watching her in her crisis I saw, as if surveying a family tree, the bareness of her life.

The elevator lowered itself on its rope, and other people got on. Lydie threw me a look. She was weary, but she held my eyes for just a beat too long. It was like a definite squeeze in a handshake. It seemed to me that my allegiance to Lydie was being consecrated in blood—in the metallic tincture of the elevator air, where speaking was basically forbidden, I was committing to discretion in matters that went out uncontainably up through floors of the hospital and down, into and throughout Tulsa. Exiting the lobby, Lydie leaned on me and gripped my arm with her unpainted nails and we proceeded, like a Boy Scout and an old lady, across the street.

"You know Lydie," I told her, while I thought she was in my power, "Adrienne loved you."

She didn't answer me until we got in my car. "I always told people that Adrienne was the reason I didn't have any children. Now. We're going to go buy flowers."

She gave me directions. I didn't know why other people wouldn't be sending flowers; the family isn't supposed to get the flowers. But I didn't say anything. There was to be a gathering at the Booker tonight. "It's what people expect," she said. "We did it this way when my uncle died."

I was her personal assistant now, I realized.

The sun had come out, and the sand under my eyes was clogged with tears, and every time I blinked I wished it was to sleep. At each stoplight I took my hands off the wheel and rubbed at my eyes and rested until the light turned green. I was exhausted. "How is Rod?" I asked.

"When Rod had a child, it was so strange. I thought: Oh, I'm glad someone is at least going to keep the family going. But we stopped thinking of her that way years ago, Jim."

"That she wasn't interested in the family business."

"You understand."

"But Rod wasn't either," I said.

"He wishes he had been." Lydie's voice was trembling. "You know—have you noticed? He never really knew her."

I drove upright, like a loyal chauffeur.

"You know one thing you can do for me, Jim Praley?" She regained her voice, its drawl. "Talk Rod into coming tonight."

"I will."

"He's going to fly away, you know, and he's never going to come back."

The florist-cum-nursery Lydie directed me to was a landmark in Tulsa; it featured a two-story neon rose—the kind of landmark that gets shown after an apocalypse, smoking and twisted. Adrienne and I often drove by here—and I resented Lydie, for a second, for picking this out of all of Tulsa's flower shops.

She opened her door, but then waited. "Jim," she said, as I helped her up, "you've got to steady me."

She was leaning quite emphatically on my arm. My

biceps twitched. In the milky light of the nursery, her sad smile looked almost drugged. "What do we get?" I asked.

"Profusions," she said.

I set her down on a folding chair that the clerk had very observantly presented.

"Profusions," I said. I walked up and down the aisles, trying to focus. The humidity, combined with the stink of fertilizer, shrouded my thoughts, and I wandered far to the end of the greenhouse. I wanted to be alone.

In a corner, among the succulents, I found an orange flower that looked right—thumb-high, waxen. It fit Adrienne, I felt, her spirit of ungirliness, but it had nothing to do with a funeral. It was a flower for someone to keep at their bedside and tend. It would look precious if I got it now—Lydie might perhaps love for me to bring her such a flower and say it was "from me." But the relationship I wanted with Lydie was otherwise. I scooped up three buckets of cut carnations and turned to the cash register, all business, but there Lydie was, arms out like a forklift. She took the flowers. "Get those others too," she said. And she told the clerk about her niece as she paid.

I found the necktie sack. Someone in the waiting room had tucked it behind a couch pushed up against a window: as if it needed to be pinned there.

This stiff blue sack with floppy golden cords. It embarrassed me in precisely the way I had known it would.

Wanting to get a few of my things out of Adrienne's room, I stopped at the nurses' desk, timidly, to ask if Room 607 had been cleaned.

I found Rod bent over his suitcase, packing up to go. Lydie had told me he would be filling out forms all afternoon—she had sent her lawyer, Gilbert Lee, to help him. Lydie was probably going to sue the hospital, she had told me.

"Jim." Rod put his hand on my shoulder. "You heard?" His voice was clotted.

"Yes," I said. I tried to know what to say. It was like I was wearing seven satchels and camera bags and had to open each flap and rummage in them to try to find what I was supposed to feel.

"All the others were here," he said, referring I assumed to Jenny and Nic and everyone else who had probably been a half hour behind me on their way from the diner.

"What was that like?" I asked.

Rod returned to his bags. "They're going to stage a benefit concert, they said. I don't know to benefit what."

The room became very small, and seemed to stink. "Are you going tonight, to the penthouse?"

He shook his head.

"It would really mean a lot to Lydie if you came."

He stood up and gave me a look. "Jim. You can work for Lydie if you want, but don't go thinking she's a saint."

He turned his huge clutched face and bent back to his packing.

I had intended to spend the afternoon at the Rose Garden at Woodward Park. I thought that with my good shoes on, the paths of gravel would feel almost French— one thinks of French poetry, so conversational, yet firm and remorseless: good for thinking about death.

Instead I holed up in the intensive-care waiting area, where I had first found Rod two days ago, and where I had left my big green bag all that time. I sat with my green bag on my lap. What if Rod was still coming to us? I thought. What if he was only on his way now, now that she had died? What if he had arrived only now, and had asked me—or someone in my place—to take him around town, to show him all the venues of Adrienne's life? Indeed, what if I wasn't even here yet? But was on my way now, now that she had died?

It was like I needed to think. But it wasn't even thinking. My body produced a kind of sadness, and I found it comfortable to sit in that.

Up in the Booker, we sat in conversation, the family group. When I arrived and the elevator doors parted, my green walls of memory, the horse painting, and all the penthouse furniture confronted me. Lydie herself assumed the antler-backed chair, and pointed to a stool for me. About a dozen others sat around. Carrie Fitzgerald stood in a corner, on the phone, in a black kimono. Rod was absent. Everyone, especially two or three elderly women, seemed to be there on the basis of connections established in previous generations, and our flowers, fittingly arranged here and there, did seem to be just the thing.

"We can be thankful that your uncle isn't alive to see this," said one of the older women.

Lydie smiled tightly and passed a bowl of hard candies.

"Margey said she'd be here by seven . . . ," put in one of the younger women.

There were sarcastic smiles all around, and comments. Margey was Margaret Cann, the mayor.

Lydie was going to sue the hospital. That was affirmed, and the little old ladies nodded solemnly. "What we're all feeling . . . ," Lydie began. She feigned hesitation, shying her nose back from the coffee table. "Before Margey gets here," she said. "What we're all feeling is a sense of lost opportunity. There isn't anyone in this room I haven't gone to at some time for advice about Adrienne. We deplored the choices she made. But I think all of us, if we remember, always watched for her to"—Lydie paused—"come back to us. We hoped that when the crisis came, it might be the turning point. Because we always knew there would be a crisis. But we were never prepared for this."

There was something in these words that revealed a most un-Lydie-like desperation. I believed at least some of Lydie's erratic behavior that morning had been real—Adrienne meant more to her than she wanted to admit; as she spoke I caught glances crisscrossing the room that indicated as much. Lydie was not usually like this. Her head was drooping, actually. There was something in there, a maternal egg that was all catastrophically hatching.

I wondered what these old women really thought. For them Lydie herself was prodigal: unmarried, hectic, the flotsam of a dynasty. Her life had been a long exercise in coping. But Lydie caught me staring, mooning at her, and I excused myself. I walked out onto the terrace to think.

Nowhere in the Booker tonight, coming up the elevator or in the penthouse, had I been able to detect the presence of Adrienne. Now I walked from one end of the terrace to the other, trying to stir up memories. The tower across the way, the subject of so much drunken staring when I was young, looked like nothing but a blown-up photograph, a random chunk of skyline. It was inert and bright. I had cried too much already. I bridled at the idea that Adrienne's life was a waste of time—"a lost opportunity." But it was true that we had dreamed of a crisis—a way to break open the future. It felt like bad luck to be up on the terrace. The only thing I liked was the breeze—always a little pushy at that height.

Through the glass I heard a commotion, and looked back in. This must be the mayor was here. I could see her face, trapped up on Lydie's shoulder. They were hugging; the mayor bit her lip, and then was let down, shortish, with large bobbed hair and blocky, smart-lady earrings. She knocked around the room robotically, straight-necked but quick to hug, bumping into everyone. Her smile was almost one of gratitude: hug, hug, hug.

I let myself back inside, to be introduced. Lydie did the honors: "This is Jim Praley. He's moving back home from New York and is going to join Booker Petroleum. An old friend of Adrienne's."

"Did you know Adrienne well?"

"Yeah." I rose on my tiptoes. I was surprised that Lydie had walked off and left me with the mayor.

"I never got to meet her," the mayor was explaining. "But Lydie is such an important friend."

"Adrienne was very popular with the youth."

The mayor nodded slowly, unsure of what to say.

"She was a nexus for the arts scene, networking between Albert Dooney and all the kids in the Brady District."

The mayor still didn't know what to do with this information. She was staring past me, at a piece of carpet near the bedroom. "I used to live with her, basically, in that bedroom," I said.

The elevator dinged, and a young girl wearing a small black turban peeked out. She looked like she had come to the wrong party. But then Jenny followed, and then a whole carful of kids stepped out onto the carpet. They had gathered at Albert's and come here en masse. They all wore black. Rather than bewildered by this terribly real, real-world situation, they seemed to feel in their bones that their moment had come. The first elevator load lined up to offer Lydie their condolences, like kids congratulating the enemy's coach. Albert broke off and came over to me and shook my hand, having recognized me. But the elevator dinged again, and again, and the room grew noisy, and soon the majority of the people in the room were kids. People wanted to hug; Nic, looking at table legs, let me keep my arm draped around his shoulders while we talked. "Does the family not want us here?" Jenny asked me. Jenny had on a very adult black dress; she had just bought it this afternoon, she told me. I imagined her going to the mall: with what sense of purpose she parked her car in the Promenade Mall parking garage and strode into Dillard's.

They were not having a *benefit* concert for Adrienne, but a memorial. "You write poetry, don't you?" They wanted me to read. Of course I declined; I disentangled myself from the kids and made for the adults again. But it was a real consolation to me, that they were going to organize something.

I was at the drinks table with Carrie Fitzgerald. Her kimono sleeves threatened to drag through the canapés and I offered to pour for her. "It's such a remarkable group of kids," Carrie said, holding her glass. "I'm so glad that they could all be here."

"So am I."

"When Chase and Adrienne were little, she was so shy. She would come over to play with Chase but he wouldn't know where she was. She would be hiding for hours and hours, somewhere in the house, and we got to where we wouldn't look for her, we'd just wait for her to make her reappearance, you know. She was like a little demon. And now all these people love her."

I liked Carrie for saying this. I thought I couldn't add anything. But Carrie kept looking at me with her big, watery, fortysomething eyes. So I spoke: "This gathering didn't really mean much, to me, until the kids arrived."

"I felt that way too," said Carrie. She was going to cry.

I quickly asked, "Have you talked to Chase?"

She closed her eyes and nodded. "Yes." Her voice was croaky. "He should be on his way from the airport now. He said—" Carried blinked, and cleared her face. "Well, there's a group of young people out there who're all from Tulsa, who always meet for brunch, with him and Adrienne. And he said they all wanted to come, if there was a funeral."

That was very hard for me to hear. "Chase is really so great," I said, and left.

Back towards Lydie's group I heard them still saying that Adrienne had been "on a path" towards this, and that one might "have expected it." I didn't hear Lydie say anything, and couldn't tell whether it was all ratified by her, or whether she was getting very softly boxed in and blamed.

"Listen, Lydie," I said, taking the liberty of sitting down. "There's something I can tell you about."

Lydie's eyeliner up close looked purple, her eyes swollen. "I was worried about what you said earlier." I got off the couch and squatted by her arm. "I don't want you to think that she wasn't happy. Adrienne missed a lot of opportunities, it's true. But when she was alive—" I formed my fingers in a gesture of connoisseurship. "Adrienne really achieved something. It's the point. You know she became the person she wanted to be."

"Of course Jim."

"I mean that to be a comfort to you."

Her mouth looked strangled. "Okay Jim."

But it was a matter of Lydie being sufficiently taken with me to take my point. And I saw that she wasn't sufficiently taken.

It wasn't until I looked up though, and saw Chase coming out from the elevator, that I could be sure any of us were going to get what we deserved. I finally felt a thrill of justice, of fittingness. The elevator had not dinged in some time, and then we looked, and the doors parted to reveal Chase Fitzpatrick. He had come straight from the airport. He entered the room like a grim Luke Skywalker, dressed in black, and in black boots, bending his blond mop to take his friends in hand: he came in taking everyone's hand and murmuring, ashen-faced. He had gotten on a plane. It made a great difference to me to behold him. With him my sense of moment was almost answered.

It was in trouble that I acquired my taste for parties: people parting and classes graduating. Or parties that are illegal. In college and occasionally in New York, you find a party that is deeply defined. Usually by loss. Such is the magic of social promotion, as practiced at the nation's universities—each year the end of an era. It was with a veteran's sure hand that I reached out at the penthouse for Jenny, who was standing nearby. "Were you going to go out on the terrace and smoke?" I asked. She thought I wanted to avoid Chase. But it was because I knew how to arrange things that I wanted to let him greet everyone else first, while I waited out in the open air.

The terrace seemed chilly, and I gave Jenny my jacket. She put her arms through its sleeves. We lit two of her cigarettes, and after a couple of puffs stepped closer and held each other, side by side. When I coughed, she could probably feel my ribs. "I don't usually smoke," I said.

Word of Lydie's lawsuit had reached the kids, and Jenny wanted to discuss. I refused. "Tell me about college," I said.

Jenny looked up from my shoulder. To kiss Jenny would have filled me with joy. "I actually didn't know you smoked," she said.

I shrugged. "I'd like to pretend to smoke, sort of." I held the smoking cigarette out over the guardrail, and worked my jaw. "There are lots of things, where it was at

244

the beginning of my adult life when I dated Adrienne, and then I wish she could see me now, because I'm different. I have so much energy sometimes when I'm out, when everybody goes home, and I take my subway like I own it you know with my arms flung out over the seats, waiting for anybody else to get on board. The doors open at every stop. So it's Adrienne who could get on board. Who would see me—and being beheld by her is what I'm trying to prepare for, all the time. Or that's basically what I do in my head, when nothing else's happening."

"Like you're talking to her," Jenny murmured.

"Like I'm getting ready for a test."

By the time Chase found us, we had accomplished an impressive silence: at least Jenny and I stared down from the same height, and had the same perspective, leaning on that rail with our shoulders hunched almost in a shrug, stories above the sedate night streets of Tulsa.

Chase had been out on the terrace for a while first—he had been detained by some guys by the door. But he got away and he made straight for us.

I turned around without his having to say anything. We hugged. It was Jenny who remarked on the moment: "I can't believe I'm seeing this," she said. My sense of drama had been contagious.

"Jim Praley." Chase bit his lip and gripped my shoulder, rubbing a fist into my belly. He was crying in a dispersed, ongoing way, talking as cheerfully as possible with the general smear of tears on his face. "It restored a little of my faith in the universe when I heard that you were here."

I tried to smile properly; I wanted to give myself

away. It was not so much that we were rivals. It was that Chase was her lifelong friend, he represented the whole backside of her life, and I had failed to love him.

"Jim Praley."

His voice faltered, and I moved to take him by the arm, and led us around to a table I remembered, still there, still bolted into place in an alcove with two chairs. "You two sit," Jenny said. She preferred to lean back in the shadows, out of the wind.

Once seated, Chase sighed. He was looking at his hands, moving them over the surface of the table as if trying to straighten a stack of papers. "Jim Praley." He looked up. "You were even going to take off a year from college."

"Did you know about that?"

"It was a big deal."

Maybe Chase sat down with me because he thought I was owed that much: he recognized my unique standing with Adrienne.

"So you were here for the last couple of days?" he asked.

He wanted me to talk. I told Chase the truth: I had seen his mass email. "I don't know why, it was just like I knew, and I got on a plane. I've been incredibly blessed to be here," I said. I reached out to Chase across the table. But he kept his hands in his lap.

"So I was here for the last two nights. Rod and I sat up together the first night—it was interesting to meet him. But you know all about him—and your mom was there too, that night. Adrienne was completely uncon-scious. I talked to Nic a bit about the accident—you know all about that too—I was impressed by the idea though, what Nic said, that when Adrienne got on her motorcycle, the reason she crashed was that she forgot the road had been changed. That she was following the old road, on autopilot I guess, but I would put it another way. I would say she was going on old feelings."

I glanced at Chase; his face seemed marble, his eyes averted. I leaned in more, and tented my hands at the center of the table. "And then I was there when she woke up last night. She wasn't coherent for me. But she was present—"

"She was probably in great pain."

"Yep."

Jenny stepped out of the shadows; she had started crying. Chase beckoned for her, wanting her to be included. She knelt beside the table, and Chase took her hand. She reached for mine too, and held it. But Chase and I remained apart, in our opposite seats.

I looked at him. "Thank you Chase," I said simply.

With his free hand, he made a heavy gesture, waving away the air between us. "No regrets," he said. He said it a second time: "No regrets."

Jenny was speaking through her tears. "We're going to go dancing later, is that what you heard, Chase?"

Chase looked up. "Do you think Adrienne would approve of that, Jim?"

"I definitely do."

"Okay then," he said.

But none of us were going to go dancing. Chase was lost, staring into corridors inside of himself. He wouldn't get over this, I could guess, for a long, long time.

We three rose and went in. Kim had already texted me to say that she was here, and now I looked for her in the crowd. As I approached I heard her say the words "blood clot" and "blood thinner"; she and her neighbor were conscientiously discussing the cause of death. Kim and I decided we had to look some of this medical information up on the internet, and so I showed her into the study. "There used to be a computer in here," I said. The study was the same—windowless. "Okay," I said. It was actually the same computer as before, an ancient 286. Awesomely grim, to be confronted with this machine. I sat down and switched it on—the CPU first, and then monitor.

"It's old," said Kim.

It was booting from DOS. The RAM counted itself, and then the green type flew up the monitor, scrolling fast, and halting, as if stuck. Kim laid her hand on my shoulder. I kept my eyes on the monitor. "She would have been very happy that you came back," whispered Kim.

Windows loaded, and then I clicked on the browser. "Maybe Lydie knows the password," I suggested. Kim left to go ask.

My legs were like the legs of crabs. The room spun, the 1980s office chair squeaked. On my second pass I stopped: I saw the pulsing light of a laptop there on the floor.

The laptop was asleep.

I watched the light pulse, like an EKG. It was a newish laptop.

I wondered whose it was.

Without opening the laptop, without touching it, I crept out of the study and cut back through the party

248

and into the bedroom. The bed, the furniture, everything was museum-perfect—totally as if Adrienne had never lived here. But then in the private bath, through the shower door, I thought I saw products: pastel and bright green bottles behind the rippled glass. I opened the medicine cabinet: cotton balls and dainty scissors, more products, all jumbled together not by use, but by a hurried maid. New things, unexpired things. Face cream, open. A pill bottle with a clean laser-printed label, dated this April 18. So she had been back here, maybe. On retreats from L.A. sometimes—giving herself residencies in Tulsa. Having hermitages up here. That's how I would have been. A pedestrian again. Haunting the streets.

I washed my hands urgently. Then, lifting up the bed skirt, I peered under the bed and found a pair of red espadrilles. They were worn to the heel. I fished one out and pressed the insole. It was soft as her toe.

In defiance of any onlookers from in the main room, I went to stand before the doors of the big master wardrobe and pulled them wide. Here was the end of the rainbow: black, black, black, fuzzing into gold and silver sweaters and then breaking into turquoise white yellow red, hanging. I slid my fingers between separate hangers: a tie shirtfront dress, its halves hanging apart; a cream-colored gown with blue fleurs-de-lis; a lone magenta sash, hanging; four men's oxford shirts, all yellow, soft with wear; a waitress's dress I remembered, with MILDRED embroidered above a steaming apple pie. I had suppressed all memory of such a dress, but I knew it. She had worn it to a party once.

I knew half these dresses. Oh God. I racked through

them: another strapless gown, gray, with a tall elastic waist; a gold sequined blouse that looked like chain mail and that had a rip I remembered—and I found it with my fingers, at the armpit; a blue dress with a flounced hemline, causing me to look down. At shoes: the usual pell-mell, heels chopped up like waves at sea, every color, and busted espadrilles stacked in the corner. So she continued to walk everywhere. She came back here sometimes, and walked the old streets. Some of the shoes were very ancient, like dead bats, equally gothic as the fashion used to be, but at least one flat that I saw, mateless on the surface of the pile, had to be almost brand-new: it had a certain kind of notch, for toe cleavage, that I had seen on fashionable girls in New York that summer. A dull object caught my eye. I knelt down. It was an old beat-up boot with weeping laces. My old hiking boot from Boy Scouts.

I had stood up, and was holding the boot as I might hold a model boat: a hand at bow and a hand at stern, right up close to my face.

"Yeah, no, it's apparently pretty normal in spinal cord cases." Kim had gotten online. She looked a little beautiful, paused in the doorway. Standing with one foot forward and the other foot back.

"I guess I'm going to take off," I said. Kim moved out of my way. Near the elevators I spotted Lydie. She was seeing the mayor out, and I decided to descend on her, while I still had this look of profundity on my face.

We smiled, and shook hands in silence. I spoke gently. "I'm going back to New York, Lydie."

She kind of curtseyed. "Okay Jim."

"Thank you though for—"

She smiled weakly. "Go," she said. I turned; I was going to catch the mayor's elevator car. "But Jim," called Lydie, "where did you get that shoe?"

I was still holding the boot. I turned to put it back. But instead of returning it to the wardrobe, I slid into the kitchen, squeezing past a group of girls. Under the pretext of getting a beer, I opened the refrigerator and put the boot inside. I saw uneaten sushi, bitters, limes turned brown, and a sheaf of unshucked corn. I saw her everywhere—the magnets from SoundBiz on the refrigerator door; and her doodling on a menu, angry geometric shapes. I opened one of the drawers, loud on its casters. "Is there a bottle opener?" I asked aloud, for the benefit of the girls standing near me. But I never was going to drink this beer: I rooted through more menus, rubber bands, screwdrivers, as quietly as I could, until I found a little beaded pouch I knew, and inside it felt the familiar weight of Adrienne's extra key. It was the spare key, one of the long-toothed keys that opened Adrienne's studio. Right where I knew it was.

And then I wound back around the corner and pressed the arrow down.

I wanted to walk our old walk. I came down from the penthouse and plunged out the lobby doors into the night that, back in the nineties, had used to be day, when we set out on our mornings. Indeed the door of the lobby felt a little light under my arm, and I was afraid I might break it. And when I got out into the middle of the street and looked up, I expected the skyscrapers to not be there. I was trying to deprive myself of Tulsa all at once. But the black towers stood there, and the street was bland beneath my feet. It was real, and beyond it the boring neighborhoods were realer.

The wind tore through the cross streets like a gale from the deserts—streaming out to western Oklahoma and Texas and Mexico beyond. I remembered how the skyscrapers used to look from my parents' car: the lungs of my hometown, combusting and bright. The engine of the known world.

So I had needed Adrienne as a memory. When people heard I was from Tulsa, they expected stories, and I too, as I walked around on the East Coast, saw how cool it could be to be from here. Even when I was a little boy I knew what an origin story was. But Tulsa was mute. When I met Adrienne I knew what I needed. And as soon as I had it from her I instantly turned back to my own life, and built up a young man who merely carried Adrienne in his heart, as an image. Now I wanted to give Adrienne back to herself.

But she was dead, and so I was going to get to keep her forever.

I walked over the tracks, didn't glance at the Center of the Universe, but hid myself among the warehouses of the Brady District. On my peregrinations the afternoon before I'd never made it over onto these streets. So here they were, still packed up in darkness, just as I had left them five years ago. I could hear the bar crowds down the street, a rebuke to me, and I hurried by; on the sidewalk in front of Adrienne's studio I stopped with my back to the door and looked both ways. The long-toothed key still grabbed in the lock—I jogged up the steps—and the flashlight still hung on its string.

And its batteries worked. I shined the flashlight around, and in my heart I panicked. I felt like I was inspecting the scene of a crime. I didn't see any easels, only old music gear. A microphone left out, getting dusty. Finally, a lamp. I switched it on and saw the clothing rack, stocked with some things, khaki high-waisted shorts clipped up on a hanger, and at least three or four hanging bags of dry cleaning. I went up and checked the stapled receipts: transactions from only one week ago. And I saw a bed. I wondered at what point did she decide it was all right to sleep here. We never slept here. This was a defeat in her life, a slippage. The top sheet ran twisted, hanging off the side like a rope, the pillows were on the floor. Reaching down before I could stop myself, I touched one of those pillows, I picked it up like a professional basketball player picks up a basketball: one-handed.

I made that bed. It was a ritual in grief. And also a daily ritual, one that Adrienne never took notice of when she was alive. Perfect. I patted up the pillows but didn't know where to put them, so I put them back on the floor, then I pulled the mattress pad tight and drew the sheet up to its edge. I pulled it very straight. Then I replaced the pillows and threw the blanket over all of it, coming around to each corner to correct it and to check the sheet. Perfect. Perfect.

Somebody would come in here soon, looking after Adrienne's things—and when they noticed the neat, tight bed, if they knew Adrienne at all, they would know that she hadn't made it. That I had been here, maybe—and then I noticed the Advil on the bedside table, and again an old medicine bottle, this one quite old, stuffed with weed, her name printed in dot matrix: "Booker, Adrienne." So she never became famous.

Idly, I opened the bedside drawer, and saw one revolver pointing back at me.

I picked it up. Had the safety been off this whole time? I inspected the chamber. Three bullets. I bent over and cried. That's exactly how many should have been left, after we shot out the window.

I stuck it out and aimed: A salute, as if. An apology. I was apparently too old for grand gestures. Pretending to aim, I waved the gun at the window, waved it at the image of the refracted streetlight. I crooked the gun in my lap and turned out all the bullets.

I dream sometimes that Adrienne is singing, and that I try to sing too. Sometimes she's in jail, and we have five minutes together in a bleak reception room, beneath a high window. Sometimes we're onstage. And we try to sing a duet, with the spotlight in our faces and with all of the Tulsa people there in the heave of the audience. I dream how brave I would have to be to stick my vocal cords out there and let them wave and vibrate, next to Adrienne's. Merle Haggard said recently in an interview that to sing with your wife, "actually singing together, actually harmonizing together, that requires some dual fault that might not exist in other marriages." I think he meant that he and his wife had each done something wrong, and had each confessed it. And therefore weren't afraid to open up, to sing in each other's faces.

So the burden of my nightmare could be this: that I never really opened up to Adrienne. I never confessed. I worshipped her but I sacrificed nothing. I dated her the whole time like a little kid who doesn't want anybody to see what he's reading. Adrienne got so eager every time I started telling about my parents, or about my writing. I remember her sitting Indian-style on that whitework bedspread gripping her socked feet out of sheer attentiveness while I told her, for example, about the time my mother found my poetry. The admixture of shame I felt, having written what I had written, and not being willing to explain it to my mother. To Adrienne, that aroused her faithful pity, I think. But I never really let Adrienne counsel me on such matters. I never realized how clearly she perceived my embarrassment. I shoved my embarrassment back into my bag, and turned around, and then expected Adrienne to educate me.

You know I used to belabor the real memories: the bitter way Adrienne smoked when she was tired; the offhand, superior way she ate with her fingers, discarding chicken bones off from her plate; the way she walked into a crowded party acting as if nobody were there. She had a tiny belt she used to wear that, when she was sitting, talking, she would idly whip off and thread around her wrists in a figure eight, like to handcuff herself. There was once in my car when we were making out we thrashed around so showily that we got our feet up by the headrest and our heads on the floor mat, kissing fast so as not to have to remark on our predicament, I think we both liked the idea of that floor mat that had shoe dirt spread into it and smelled like plastic with our own wine smell. Sometimes when we stood up in the mornings in the penthouse it was as if we had borne that bad party smell up there just to go out on the terrace and let the wind rip it off. And most of the time we weren't at parties: I was watching Adrienne paint, and she stood there like a practiced girl, used to being watched, about to dive off the high board for hours, with the raw canvas in front of her and her Tulsa-purchased studio warming up, all the time.

But what I tend to think about more, now (and I don't see any reason why this will change), is the years away. When I might have been wiser. Had I come to find her. When I was in New York. And she was on her way to L.A.

Which is simply to say that those years when we were apart, but both alive, were the sweetest. Because they had the most potential. And I think in my dream it's those years that we force open and would sing, if we could.

But sometimes when I'm at work and I get tired, I think—and I really do believe: only the famous people, the people you listen to all your life, really have it, can really sing. Adrienne tried. For all our studies we had no idea.

ACKNOWLEDGMENTS

Thanks first to my agent, Edward Orloff, for seeing this book clear. To my editor, Allison Lorentzen, for her commitment and her strength. To early readers Karan Mahajan and Ida Hattemer-Higgins, for their confidence. To other readers: Maureen Chun, Ceridwen Dovey, Sam Munson, Amelia Lester, Roy Scranton, and Willing Davidson. To Taylor Sperry and others at Penguin. A tip of my hat to Priscilla Becker, Ellery Washington, Thad Ziolkowski, Julia Holmes, Timothy Farrington, Claire Aaronson, Adam Berlin, and John Berlin, each of whom made some unconscious contribution to this book in a conversation I still remember. Thanks to my aunt Linda for her interest, to my aunt Nell for her precedent. To Arlen and Clara Gill for their love. I also want to thank Rachel Cohen here, for her early mentorship.

Thanks to Dinaw Mengestu, for letting me sit at his table.

Thanks to my mother and father, whose love and grace allow me to be who I am. And to my brother Sam, for his grace.

This book is dedicated to my wife, Annie Bourneuf. She keeps a roof over my head; she wakes me up in the morning. She knows what I know.